Anna

Enjoy the world of nature, it really is wonderful !

Much love

Godfather Martin

x x x

What a Wonderful World!

All things bright and beautiful,
All creatures great and small,
All things wise and wonderful,
The Lord God made them all.

CECIL FRANCES ALEXANDER (1818–95)

What a Wonderful World!

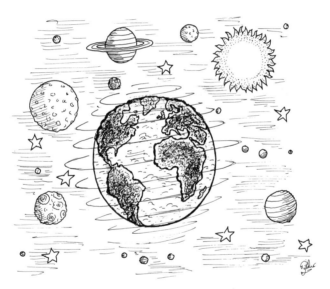

A Special Collection
compiled by Pat Alexander

Illustrated by Pythia Ashton-Jewell

A LION BOOK

Selection, arrangement and introductory material
copyright © 1998 Pat Alexander
Illustrations copyright © 1998 Pythia Ashton-Jewell
This edition copyright © 1998 Lion Publishing

Published by
Lion Publishing
Sandy Lane West, Oxford, England
ISBN 0 7459 3831 0

First edition 1998
10 9 8 7 6 5 4 3 2 1 0

A catalogue record for this book is available
from the British Library

Typeset in Latin 725

Printed and bound in Spain

Contents

1
Long, Long Ago

We live in a wonderful world. But where did it
come from? How did it begin?
No one was there to tell us. But people everywhere have told
stories about it. Best-known of all is the Bible's story, so I have
begun with that. In the story from *The Magician's Nephew*,
C.S. Lewis tells how another world, Narnia, began.
And in *Haffertee and the Picture Pattern*, for younger readers,
a soft-toy hamster finds out how he was made.

The Making

From *My Own Book of Bible Stories*

PAT ALEXANDER

This story comes from the first book of the Bible,
Genesis, chapters 1 and 2.

Long, long ago there was no world – no sky, no sea, no land, no people.

In the beginning, God made the universe. It was completely dark. There was no sound to be heard.

Then, out of the darkness, breaking the silence, God spoke.

'Let there be light!' God said. And there was light. The light was good. God called it 'day', and kept the dark for night. That was the first day.

Then God said, 'Let there be space around the world!' And it was so. God called the space around the world 'sky'. That was the second day.

Then God said, 'Let all the water come together away from the land!' And it was so. God called the land 'earth' and the water 'sea'.

And God saw that it was good.

But the land was brown and bare. Nothing grew. So God said, 'Let there be all kinds of plants and trees!' And the world became green with growing things – fruit and flowers and vegetables.

And God saw that it was good. That was the third day.

Then God said, 'Let there be lights in the sky to shine on the earth by day and night!' And it was so. One of the lights he called 'sun' – that was for the daytime. The other he called 'moon' – that was for the night-time. He made the twinkling stars.

And God saw that it was good. That was the fourth day.

Then God said, 'Let there be fish in the sea and birds in the air!' God made all kinds of water creatures, big and small, from the monster whale to the tiniest crab. He made all kinds of birds, big and small, from the great albatross to the tiniest humming-bird.

Sparrows too! The fish splashed and the birds sang and the world was alive with sound.

And God saw that it was good. 'Let the fish fill the sea. Let the birds lay eggs and have chicks,' he said, 'and fill the world.' That was the fifth day.

Then God said, 'Let the earth produce all kinds of animals, wild and tame, big and small!' And it was so. God made them all and he saw that it was good.

'Now,' God said, 'the world is ready. Let there be people! They will be like me. And I shall put them in charge of all the creatures I have made.'

So God made people. He made them like himself. He made man and woman: Adam and Eve.

'You are to have children,' he said, 'to live in every part of the world. And I am putting you in charge of everything: the water and the land, the plants and the fish and the birds and the animals. They are all yours. Look after them for me.'

God saw all that he had made and it was very good. That was the sixth day.

So the whole universe was finished. And on the seventh day God did no work. He rested and enjoyed it all. That is why God made the seventh day a special day, for ever.

'What in the World is the Wide, Wide World?'

NORMAN STONE

What in the world is the wide wide world
O what is the wide wide world?
The wide wide world is a world God given,
Made by God for us to live in,
Given by God to be our home,
This is the wide wide world.

But what in the world is the world made of
O what in the wide wide world?
Well, it's made of rocks and stones and boulders,
Made of soil and sand and mud,
Sandstone, redstone, limestone, gritstone,
Chalk and clay and lots of wood
From the trees in the wide wide world.

And lots of the world is covered in water,
Lots of seas and lots of lakes,
With lots of fishes, turtles, whales,
Sticklebacks, frogs and sharks and snails,
All swimming in the wide wide world.

And on the land are hills and mountains,
Deserts, valleys, flatland too.
Lots of grass and lots of flowers,
Lots of trees with lots of birds in,
Eagles, robins, parrots, thrushes,
Flying round the wide wide world.

And lots and lots of different animals,
Elephants, hedgehogs, dogs and fleas,
Some in ones and twos and threes,
Some with noses, some with knees.
How many animals can you see,
When you walk round the wide wide world?

And what in the world are we to do here?
What in the wide wide world?
Well we're in charge of the wide wide world
And there's lots and lots to do...
We plant our seeds and grow our crops,
We build our houses, towns and shops
And take good care of the wide wide world
With its colours and smells and tastes and sounds
And everything else that's all around.

Then we look at the wide wide world and say,
Thank you God for another day,
As we learn and grow and sing and play
In the world you've given us for our home –
THANKS
for the wide wide world.

The Founding of Narnia

From *The Magician's Nephew*

C.S. LEWIS

*In this story we meet Polly and Digory and his unpleasant Uncle
Andrew. Some special rings Uncle Andrew has invented have
brought them to a strange new world – and with them a Cabby
and his horse Strawberry and the terrifying Witch, Queen Jardis
of Charn. If you have read* The Lion, the Witch and the
Wardrobe, *you will know about the Lion already.*

In the darkness something was happening at last. A voice had begun
to sing. It was very far away and Digory found it hard to decide from
what direction it was coming. Sometimes it seemed to come from all
directions at once. Sometimes he almost thought it was coming out
of the earth beneath them. Its lower notes were deep enough to be
the voice of the earth herself. There were no words. There was hardly
even a tune. But it was, beyond comparison, the most beautiful noise
he had ever heard. It was so beautiful he could hardly bear it. The
horse seemed to like it too: he gave the sort of whinny a horse would
give if, after years of being a cab-horse, it found itself back in the old
field where it had played as a foal, and saw someone whom it
remembered and loved coming across the field to bring it a lump
of sugar.

'Gawd!' said the Cabby. 'Ain't it lovely?'

Then two wonders happened at the same moment. One was that
the voice was suddenly joined by other voices; more voices than you
could possibly count. They were in harmony with it, but far higher
up the scale: cold, tingling, silvery voices. The second wonder was
that the blackness overhead, all at once, was blazing with stars. They
didn't come out gently one by one, as they do on a summer evening.
One moment there had been nothing but darkness; next moment a
thousand, thousand points of light leaped out – single stars,
constellations, and planets, brighter and bigger than any in our

14

world. There were no clouds. The new stars and the new voices began at exactly the same time. If you had seen and heard it, as Digory did, you would have felt quite certain that it was the stars themselves which were singing, and that it was the First Voice, the deep one, which had made them appear and made them sing.

'Glory be!' said the Cabby. 'I'd ha' been a better man all my life if I'd known there were things like this.'

The Voice on the earth was now louder and more triumphant; but the voices in the sky, after singing loudly with it for a time, began to get fainter. And now something else was happening.

Far away, and down near the horizon, the sky began to turn grey. A light wind, very fresh, began to stir. The sky, in that one place, grew slowly and steadily paler. You could see the shapes of hills, standing up dark against it. All the time the Voice went on singing.

There was soon light enough for them to see one another's faces. The Cabby and the two children had open mouths and shining eyes; they were drinking in the sound and they looked as if it reminded them of something. Uncle Andrew's mouth was open too, but not open with joy. He looked more as if his chin had simply dropped away from the rest of his face. His shoulders were stooped and his knees shook. He was not liking the Voice. If he could have got away from it by creeping into a rat's hole, he would have done so. But the Witch looked as if, in a way, she understood the music better than any of them. Her mouth was shut, her lips were pressed together, and her fists were clenched. Ever since the song began she had felt that this whole world was filled with a Magic different from hers and stronger. She hated it. She would have smashed that whole world, or all worlds, to pieces, if it would only stop the singing. The horse stood with its ears well forward, and twitching. Every now and then it snorted and stamped the ground. It no longer looked like a tired old cab-horse; you could now well believe that its father had been in battles.

The eastern sky changed from white to pink and from pink to gold. The Voice rose and rose, till all the air was shaking with it. And just as it swelled to the mightiest and most glorious sound it had yet produced, the sun arose.

Digory had never seen such a sun. The sun above the ruins of Charn had looked older than ours: this looked younger. You could imagine that it laughed for joy as it came up. And as its beams shot across the land the travellers could see for the first time what sort of place they were in. It was a valley through which a broad, swift river wound its way, flowing eastward towards the sun. Southward there were mountains, northward there were lower hills. But it was a valley of mere earth, rock and water; there was not a tree, not a bush, not a blade of grass to be seen. The earth was of many colours: they were fresh, hot, and vivid. They made you feel excited; until you saw the Singer himself, and then you forgot everything else.

It was a Lion. Huge, shaggy, and bright, it stood facing the risen sun. Its mouth was wide open in song and it was about three hundred yards away.

'This is a terrible world,' said the Witch. 'We must fly at once. Prepare the Magic.'

'I quite agree with you, Madam,' said Uncle Andrew. 'A most disagreeable place. Completely uncivilized. If only I were a younger man and had a gun – '

'Garn!' said the Cabby. 'You don't think you could shoot *'im*, do you?'

'And who *would*?' said Polly...

The Lion was pacing to and fro about that empty land and singing his new song. It was softer and more lilting than the song by which he had called up the stars and the sun; a gentle, rippling music. And as he walked and sang the valley grew green with grass. It spread out from the Lion like a pool. It ran up the sides of the little hills like a wave. In a few minutes it was creeping up the lower slopes of the distant mountains, making that young world every moment softer. The light wind could now be heard ruffling the grass. Soon there were other things besides grass. The higher slopes grew dark with heather. Patches of rougher and more bristling green appeared in the valley. Digory did not know what they were until one began coming up quite close to him. It was a little, spiky thing that threw out dozens of arms and covered these arms with green and grew larger at the rate of about an inch every two seconds. There were dozens of these things all round him now. When they were nearly as tall as himself he saw what they were. 'Trees!' he exclaimed...

Polly was finding the song more and more interesting, because she thought she was beginning to see the connexion between the music and the things that were happening. When a line of dark firs sprang up on a ridge about a hundred yards away she felt that they were connected with a series of deep, prolonged notes which the Lion had sung a second before. And when he burst into a rapid series of lighter notes she was not surprised to see primroses suddenly appearing in every direction. Thus, with an unspeakable thrill, she felt quite certain that all the things were coming (as she said) 'out of the Lion's head'. When you listened to his song you heard the things he was making up: when you looked round you, you saw them...

The Lion was singing still. But now the song had once more changed. It was more like what we should call a tune, but it was also far wilder. It made you want to run and jump and climb. It made you want to shout. It made you want to rush at other people and either hug them or fight them. It made Digory hot and red in the face. It had some effect even on Uncle Andrew... But what the song did to the two humans was nothing compared with what it was doing to the country.

Can you imagine a stretch of grassy land bubbling like water in a pot? For that is really the best description of what was happening. In all directions it was swelling into humps. They were of very different sizes, some no bigger than mole-hills, some as big as wheel-barrows, two the size of cottages. And the humps moved and swelled till they burst, and the crumbled earth poured out of them, and from each hump there came out an animal. The moles came out just as you might see a mole come out in England. The dogs came out, barking the moment their heads were free, and struggling as you've seen them do when they are getting through a narrow hole in a hedge. The stags were the queerest to watch, for of course the antlers came up a long time before the rest of them, so at first Digory thought they were trees. The frogs, who all came up near the river, went straight into it with a plop-plop and a loud croaking. The panthers, leopards and things of that sort, sat down at once to wash the loose earth off their hind quarters and then stood up against the trees to sharpen their front claws. Showers of birds came out of the trees. Butterflies fluttered. Bees got to work on the flowers as if they hadn't a second to lose. But the greatest moment of all was when the biggest hump broke like a small earthquake and out came the sloping back, the large, wise head, and the four baggy-trousered legs of an elephant. And now you could hardly hear the song of the Lion; there was so much cawing, cooing, crowing, braying, neighing, baying, barking, lowing, bleating, and trumpeting.

But though Digory could no longer hear the Lion, he could see it. It was so big and so bright that he could not take his eyes off it. The other animals did not appear to be afraid of it. Indeed, at that very moment, Digory heard the sound of hoofs from behind; a second later the old cab-horse trotted past him and joined the other beasts. (The air had apparently suited him as well as it had suited Uncle Andrew. He no longer looked like the poor, old slave he had been in London; he was picking up his feet and holding his head erect.) And now, for the first time, the Lion was quite silent. He was going to and fro among the animals. And every now and then he would go up to two of them (always two at a time) and touch their noses with his. He would touch two beavers among all the beavers, two leopards among all the leopards, one stag and one deer among all the deer, and leave the rest. Some sorts of animal he passed over altogether. But the pairs which he had touched instantly left their own kinds and followed him. At last he stood still and all the creatures whom he had touched came and stood in a wide circle around him. The others whom he had not touched began to wander away. Their noises faded gradually into the distance. The chosen beasts who remained were now utterly silent, all with their eyes fixed intently upon the Lion. The cat-like ones gave an occasional twitch of the tail but otherwise all were still. For the first time that day there was complete silence, except for the noise of running water. Digory's heart beat wildly; he knew something very solemn was going to be done…

The Lion, whose eyes never blinked, stared at the animals as hard as if he was going to burn them up with his mere stare. And gradually a change came over them. The smaller ones – the rabbits, moles and such-like – grew a good deal larger. The very big ones – you noticed it most with the elephants – grew a little smaller. Many animals sat up on their hind legs. Most put their heads on one side as if they were trying very hard to understand. The Lion opened his mouth, but no sound came from it; he was breathing out, a long, warm breath; it seemed to sway all the beasts as the wind sways a line of trees. Far overhead from beyond the veil of blue sky which hid them the stars sang again: a pure, cold, difficult music. Then there came a swift flash like fire (but it burnt nobody) either from the sky or from the Lion itself, and every drop of blood tingled in the children's bodies, and the deepest, wildest voice they had ever heard was saying:

'Narnia, Narnia, Narnia, awake. Love. Think. Speak. Be walking trees. Be talking beasts.'

Haffertee and the Picture Pattern

From *Haffertee Hamster Diamond*

JANET AND JOHN PERKINS

It all began when Yolanda (Yo) Diamond's pet hamster died.
To cheer her up, her mother (Ma Diamond) made a
ginger-and-white soft-toy hamster. The new Haffertee
Hamster is quite a character, with a lot to find out…

Haffertee Hamster was dead. Diamond Yo was so sad. School was terrible. And going home again would be even worse.

The empty cage∴ the silent wheel… and no Haffertee. What could be worse than that? How could she ever go home again?

Diamond Yo was so sad.

But she did go home again – to the empty cage and the silent wheel. And the tears came.

No Haffertee!…

But Ma Diamond was at home. She put her arm around Yo and said quietly, 'Look what I've got.'

Through her tears, Yo looked.

What a funny little fellow! Ginger and white. Almost alive he looked. Black whiskers twitching, surely. And certainly a smile on his face.

'This is a new Haffertee,' said Ma Diamond gently. 'He is only a soft toy really. I've just finished making him. You have him now, Yo, and love him.'

Yo's face brightened a little. A smile struggled through. Her hands reached out to touch.

How soft the new Haffertee felt. How cuddly!

Slowly at first, then quick and excited, she tickled his whiskers and poggled his ears.

'Haffertee,' she whispered. 'You *are* a Haffertee.'

The tears were gone now. And Haffertee and Yo were all over

the house. Yo showed him everywhere. And before they knew it, it was time for bed.

Haffertee was given a very special place inside Diamond Yo's pillowcase...

Haffertee was one of the family already. He had a new friend, too: Howl Owl, a soft toy like himself...

When Haffertee woke next morning, the first person he looked for was his friend Howl Owl.

There he was, on the shelf above the door, eyes closed. Haffertee looked all round the room.

There was a piece of paper lying on the floor. It was covered in funny drawings. And along one side Haffertee could see his own name written in big, bold black letters.

HAFFERTEE HAMSTER DIAMOND, SOFT TOY.

'That's odd,' thought Haffertee. And he pulled himself out of his pillowcase and went over to take a closer look.

He picked the paper up and looked at it this way and that way and the other way.

This way he couldn't understand it.

That way it made no sense.

And the other way was just as puzzling.

'Whatever is it?' he murmured to himself. At least, he thought it was to himself. He had not heard Howl Owl flutter down from the shelf. Howl's deep voice made him jump.

'That's a pattern,' said Howl slowly.

'Oh!' said Haffertee quickly, not liking to ask what a pattern was.

'Those are the pictures Ma Diamond used to help her cut out your pieces and put you together.'

Haffertee felt rather strange. The idea of being cut out and then put together seemed very odd.

He looked at himself carefully.

He looked at himself sideways and frontways and upwards and downwards.

He still couldn't see that he looked at all like the drawings on the paper.

'You say Ma Diamond made me?' he squeaked at last.

'Yes,' said Howl certainly. 'Ma Diamond made you. She drew these pictures of your pieces and then she cut you out. She sewed the pieces all together and she made you. And now that she has made you, she loves you.'

'Ma Diamond made me,' squeaked Haffertee again. 'Ma Diamond loves me!'

'Just like God,' said another voice, softly. 'Just like God.'

Howl and Haffertee turned together to look at the voice.

Diamond Yo was sitting up in bed. Her hair was all mixed up and she was still half asleep. 'You two make a lot of noise early on a Saturday morning. You woke me up.'

'Sorry,' said Howl slowly.

'Sorry,' said Haffertee quickly. 'But you see,' went on Haffertee in a hurry, 'I saw this piece of paper with my name on it and I couldn't understand what the pictures were. Howl has been explaining it all to me. And now you say Ma Diamond is just like God. What do you mean?'

'Well,' said Yo gently, 'Ma Diamond made you, and God made Ma Diamond. Ma Diamond loves you, and God loves Ma Diamond.'

'Ah!' said Haffertee knowingly, 'then God must be a Great Maker.'

'Yes,' said Diamond Yo, after a moment's thought. 'Yes, God is a Great Maker. He made everything and everyone.'

'My Dad'

STEVE TURNER

My dad's bigger than your dad.
My dad's as tall as the moon,
as strong as the wind,
As wide as the sky.
You should see my dad!
He's got stars in his fists.
He bends rainbows on his knee.
When he breathes, clouds move.

He's good is my dad.
You can't scare him with the dark.
You can't scare him with guns or sticks.
He makes bullies say sorry
just by staring.
Big green monsters
fall asleep on his lap.
Ghosts start haunting each other.

My dad's been everywhere
but he says he likes the world.
Earth people are fun he says.
My dad knows more than teacher.
He knows everything.
He knows what you're thinking,
even when you try to trick him
by thinking something else.
If you tell a lie
my dad says he can tell
by the look on your face.

'My Dad'

My dad's the best dad ever.
I say I love him
a million times a million
times a million times a million trillion.
My dad says he loves me
a billion trillion times more than that.

My dad likes to love.
My dad made the world.

2

Who Made a Mess?

We live in a wonderful world. But it's a world gone wrong.
What can have happened to the good new
world God made to spoil it so?
The story from the Bible tells of a test which people failed.
They chose deliberately to disobey the one rule God had
given them. Digory, in my second extract from *The Magician's
Nephew*, faces his own hard choice when Aslan sends him on a
mission. Quarrels are one of the things that spoil our world,
and *The Old Man and His Children*, a story from Africa, has
something to say about that. What a lot of questions we
would like to ask God, if only we had the chance! Well, a boy
called Sam does just that, in *Sam and the Hacker*.

'Who Made a Mess?'

STEVE TURNER

Who made a mess of the planet
And what's that bad smell in the breeze?
Who punched a hole in the ozone
And who took an axe to my trees?

Who sprayed the garden with poison
While trying to scare off a fly?
Who streaked the water with oil slicks
And who let my fish choke and die?

Who tossed that junk in the river
And who stained the fresh air with fumes?
Who tore the fields with a digger
And who blocked my favourite views?

Who's going to tidy up later
And who's going to find what you've lost?
Who's going to say that they're sorry
And who's going to carry the cost?

The Spoiling

From *My Own Book of Bible Stories*
PAT ALEXANDER

*This story comes from the first book of the Bible,
Genesis, chapters 2 and 3.*

God made a garden in Eden. It was a beautiful garden full of trees, with a river running through. God gave the garden to the man – Adam – to look after. And God brought all the animals to Adam to see what he would call them. Adam gave names to all the animals: sheep and cow, lion and tiger, rabbit and mouse. And snake.

Adam loved God. He loved the garden. He loved the animals. But he was lonely without a friend. God knew he would be – until there was a woman too. When God made Eve, Adam was completely happy. Now there was someone to talk to, someone to share things with. Everything was perfect.

But not for long.

There was one thing – only one thing – God said that Adam must not do. There was a special tree in the middle of the garden. It was called 'the-tree-of-the-knowledge-of-good-and-evil'.

'You must not eat the fruit on that tree,' God said. 'If you do, you will die.'

One day the snake, who was the slipperiest, cunningest of all God's creatures, came to Eve and began to ask her about the tree-of-the-knowledge-of-good-and-evil.

'Did God say you'd die if you ate the fruit? You won't die!' he said. 'It will make you wise, as wise as God himself. That's why he doesn't want you to cat it.'

Eve listened to the silky-smooth voice of the snake.

Eve looked at the fruit. It was so good her mouth began to water. And she wanted to be wise, like God.

Eve reached up and touched the fruit – and before she could think it was in her mouth.

She gave some to Adam, and he ate it too.

Then they both knew they had made a terrible mistake.

God had made them. He had given them everything. He was their friend. And they had deliberately disobeyed him.

That evening, when God came to the garden to see them, they hid.

But no one can hide from God.

He knew at once that they had disobeyed.

'Did you eat the fruit I told you not to eat?' God asked the man.

'The woman gave it to me,' Adam said, making excuses. 'And I ate.'

'Why did you do it?' God asked the woman.

Eve hung her head, ashamed. 'It was the snake,' she whispered, making excuses.

God punished the snake.

But Adam and Eve had to leave the garden for ever.

Everything was spoiled because the man and the woman disobeyed God.

'The Naming of the Animals'

STEVE TURNER

What would you call this animal, Adam?
He's proud and he prowls and he roars,
He's stronger than anyone else I made
His coat is the colour of straw.

What would you call this animal, Adam?
Her neck stretches up to the trees,
She has four legs as skinny as sticks
And four very knobbly knees.

What would you call this animal, Adam,
With a tube instead of a nose?
His ears are like clothes on a washing line
And he hurrumphs wherever he goes.

What would you call this animal, Adam?
Her skin is as tough as old rope,
A horn sticks up on the end of her nose
And mud is her favourite soap.

What would you call this animal, Adam?
He swoops from the sky for his lunch,
He knits his own house from branches and leaves
And swallows a mouse with a crunch.

What would you call this person, Adam?
I want her to be your best friend.
Make sure you love her with all of your heart
And stay by her side 'til the end.

Digory, the Witch and the Apple

From *The Magician's Nephew*

C.S. LEWIS

Digory's mother is very ill. He wants to take some magic fruit
from Narnia to make her well. But Aslan is not pleased with
Digory: he has brought the evil Witch into Narnia, and must
undo the wrong. So Digory is sent on a journey, far away.
He must pick an apple for Aslan from a very special garden.
Polly goes with him, and the Cabby's horse, now called Fledge,
is given wings to carry them there…

It was a wonderful ride. The big snowy mountains rose above them
in every direction. The valleys, far beneath them, were so green, and
all the streams which tumbled down from the glaciers into the main
river were so blue, that it was like flying over gigantic pieces of
jewellery. They would have liked this part of the adventure to go on
longer than it did. But quite soon they were all sniffing the air and
saying 'What is it?' and 'Did you smell something?' and 'Where's it
coming from?' For a heavenly smell, warm and golden, as if from all
the most delicious fruits and flowers of the world, was coming up to
them from somewhere ahead.

'It's coming from that valley with the lake in it,' said Fledge.

'So it is,' said Digory. 'And look! There's a green hill at the far end
of the lake. And look how blue the water is.'

'It must be the Place,' said all three.

Fledge came lower and lower in wide circles. The icy peaks rose up
higher and higher above. The air came up warmer and sweeter every
moment, so sweet that it almost brought the tears to your eyes.
Fledge was now gliding with his great wings spread out motionless
on each side, and his hoofs pawing for the ground. The steep green
hill was rushing towards them. A moment later he alighted on its
slope, a little awkwardly. The children rolled off, fell without hurting
themselves on the warm, fine grass, and stood up panting a little.

They were about three-quarters of the way up the hill, and set out at once to climb to the top. (I don't think Fledge could have managed this without his wings to balance him and to give him the help of a flutter now and then.) All round the very top of the hill ran a high wall of green turf. Inside the wall trees were growing. Their branches hung out over the wall: their leaves showed not only green but also blue and silver when the wind stirred them. When the travellers reached the top they walked nearly all the way round it outside the green wall before they found the gates: high gates of gold, fast shut, facing due east.

Up till now I think Fledge and Polly had had the idea that they would go in with Digory. But they thought so no longer. You never saw a place which was so obviously private. You could see at a glance that it belonged to someone else. Only a fool would dream of going in unless he had been sent there on very special business. Digory himself understood at once that the others wouldn't and couldn't come in with him. He went forward to the gates alone.

When he had come close up to them he saw words written on the gold with silver letters; something like this:

> *Come in by the gold gates or not at all,*
> *Take of my fruit for others or forbear.*
> *For those who steal or those who climb my wall*
> *Shall find their heart's desire and find despair.*

'*Take of my fruit for others,*' said Digory to himself. 'Well, that's what I'm going to do. It means I mustn't eat any myself, I suppose. I don't know what all that jaw in the last line is about. *Come in by the gold gates.* Well who'd want to climb a wall if he could get in by a gate! But how do the gates open?' He laid his hand on them and instantly they swung apart, opening inwards, turning on their hinges without the least noise.

Now that he could see into the place it looked more private than ever. He went in very solemnly, looking about him. Everything was very quiet inside. Even the fountain which rose near the middle of the garden made only the faintest sound. The lovely smell was all round him: it was a happy place but very serious.

He knew which was the right tree at once, partly because it stood in the very centre and partly because the great silver apples with

which it was loaded shone so and cast a light of their own down
on the shadowy places where the sunlight did not reach. He walked
straight across to it, picked an apple, and put it in the breast pocket
of his Norfolk jacket. But he couldn't help looking at it and smelling
it before he put it away.

It would have been better if he had not. A terrible thirst and
hunger came over him and a longing to taste that fruit. He put it
hastily into his pocket; but there were plenty of others. Could it be
wrong to taste one? After all, he thought, the notice on the gate
might not have been exactly an order; it might have been only a
piece of advice – and who cares about advice? Or even if it were an
order, would he be disobeying it by eating an apple? He had already
obeyed the part about taking one 'for others'.

While he was thinking of all this he happened to look up through
the branches towards the top of the tree. There, on a branch above
his head, a wonderful bird was roosting. I say 'roosting' because it
seemed almost asleep: perhaps not quite. The tiniest slit of one eye
was open. It was larger than an eagle, its breast saffron, its head
crested with scarlet, and its tail purple.

'And it just shows,' said Digory afterwards when he was telling
the story to the others, 'that you can't be too careful in these magical

places. You never know what may be watching you.' But I think Digory would not have taken an apple for himself in any case. Things like Do Not Steal were, I think, hammered into boys' heads a good deal harder in those days than they are now. Still we can never be certain.

Digory was just turning to go back to the gates when he stopped to have one last look round. He got a terrible shock. He was not alone. There, only a few yards away from him stood the Witch. She was just throwing away the core of an apple she had eaten. The juice was darker than you would expect and had made a horrid stain round her mouth. Digory guessed at once that she must have climbed in over the wall. And he began to see that there might be some sense in that last line about getting your heart's desire and getting despair along with it. For the Witch looked stronger and prouder than ever, and even, in a way, triumphant: but her face was deadly white, white as salt.

All this flashed through Digory's mind in a second; then he took to his heels and ran for the gates as hard as he could pelt; the Witch after him. As soon as he was out, the gates closed behind him of their own accord. That gave him the lead but not for long. By the time he had reached the others and was shouting out 'Quick, get on, Polly! Get up, Fledge', the Witch had climbed the wall, or vaulted over it, and was close behind him again.

'Stay where you are,' cried Digory, turning round to face her, 'or we'll all vanish. Don't come an inch nearer.'

'Foolish boy,' said the Witch. 'Why do you run from me? I mean you no harm. If you do not stop and listen to me now, you will miss some knowledge that would have made you happy all your life.'

'Well, I don't want to hear it, thanks,' said Digory. But he did.

'I know what errand you have come on,' continued the Witch. 'For it was I who was close beside you in the woods last night and heard all your counsels. You have plucked fruit in the garden yonder. You have it in your pocket now. And you are going to carry it back, untasted, to the Lion; for *him* to eat, for *him* to use. You simpleton! Do you know what that fruit is? I will tell you. It is the apple of youth, the apple of life. I know, for I have tasted it; and I feel already such changes in myself that I know I shall never grow old or die. Eat it, Boy, eat it; and you and I will both live forever and be king and queen of this whole world – or of your world, if we decide to go back there.'

'No thanks,' said Digory, 'I don't know that I care much about living on and on after everyone I know is dead. I'd rather live an ordinary time and die and go to Heaven.'

'But what about this Mother of yours whom you pretend to love so?'

'What's she got to do with it?' said Digory.

'Do you not see, Fool, that one bite of that apple would heal her? You have it in your pocket. We are here by ourselves and the Lion is far away. Use your Magic and go back to your own world. A minute later you can be at your Mother's bedside, giving her the fruit. Five minutes later you will see the colour coming back to her face. She will tell you the pain is gone. Soon she will tell you she feels stronger. Then she will fall asleep – think of that; hours of sweet natural sleep, without pain, without drugs. Next day everyone will be saying how wonderfully she has recovered. Soon she will be quite well again. All will be well again. Your home will be happy again. You will be like other boys.'

'Oh!' gasped Digory as if he had been hurt, and put his hand to his head. For he now knew that the most terrible choice lay before him.

'What has the Lion ever done for you that you should be his slave?' said the Witch. 'What can he do to you once you are back in your own world? And what would your Mother think if she knew that you *could* have taken her pain away and given her back her life and saved your Father's heart from being broken, and that you *wouldn't* – that you'd rather run messages for a wild animal in a strange world that is no business of yours?'

'I – I don't think he is a wild animal,' said Digory in a dried-up sort of voice. 'He is – I don't know – '

'Then he is something worse,' said the Witch. 'Look what he has done to you already: look how heartless he has made you. That is what he does to everyone who listens to him. Cruel, pitiless boy! You would let your own Mother die rather than – '

'Oh shut up,' said the miserable Digory, still in the same voice. 'Do you think I don't see? But I – I promised.'

'Ah, but you didn't know what you were promising. And no one here can prevent you.'

'Mother herself,' said Digory, getting the words out with difficulty, 'wouldn't like it – awfully strict about keeping promises – and not stealing – and all that sort of thing. *She'd* tell me not to do it – quick as anything – if she was here.'

'But she need never know,' said the Witch, speaking more sweetly than you would have thought anyone with so fierce a face could speak. 'You wouldn't tell her how you'd got the apple. Your Father need never know. No one in your world need know anything about this whole story. You needn't take the little girl back with you, you know.'

That was where the Witch made her fatal mistake. Of course Digory knew that Polly could get away by her own ring as easily as he could get away by his. But apparently the Witch didn't know this. And the meanness of the suggestion that he should leave Polly behind suddenly made all the other things the Witch had been saying to him sound false and hollow. And even in the midst of all his misery, his head suddenly cleared, and he said (in a different and much louder voice):

'Look here; where do *you* come into all this? Why are *you* so precious fond of *my* Mother all of a sudden? What's it got to do with you? What's your game?'

'Good for you, Digs,' whispered Polly in his ear. 'Quick! Get away *now*.' She hadn't dared to say anything all through the argument because, you see, it wasn't *her* Mother who was dying.

'Up then,' said Digory, heaving her onto Fledge's back and then scrambling up as quickly as he could. The horse spread its wings.

'Go then, Fools,' called the Witch. 'Think of me, Boy, when you lie old and weak and dying, and remember how you threw away the chance of endless youth! It won't be offered you again.'

They were already so high that they could only just hear her. Nor did the Witch waste any time gazing up at them; they saw her set off northward down the slope of the hill.

They had started early that morning and what happened in the garden had not taken very long, so that Fledge and Polly both said they would easily get back to Narnia before nightfall. Digory never spoke on the way back, and the others were shy of speaking to him. He was very sad and he wasn't even sure all the time that he had done the right thing: but whenever he remembered the shining tears in Aslan's eyes he became sure.*

All day Fledge flew steadily with untiring wings; eastward with the river to guide him, through the mountains and over the wild

* Digory saw those tears when he told Aslan how ill his mother was, so we can be sure that Aslan is going to help!

wooded hills, and then over the great waterfall and down, and down, to where the woods of Narnia were darkened by the shadow of the mighty cliff, till at last, when the sky was growing red with sunset behind them, he saw a place where many creatures were gathered together by the riverside. And soon he could see Aslan himself in the midst of them. Fledge glided down, spread out his four legs, closed his wings, and landed cantering. Then he pulled up. The children dismounted. Digory saw all the animals, dwarfs, satyrs, nymphs, and other things drawing back to the left and right to make way for him. He walked straight up to Aslan, handed him the apple and said:

'I've brought you the apple you wanted, sir.'

The Old Man and His Children

An African Tale

RETOLD BY JEAN WATSON

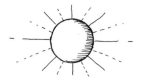

Kamau sat on his three-legged stool in the shade of the spreading mugumo tree. On its fig-like fruit, mouse-birds and green parrots were quietly feeding. The old man sat very still with his eyes closed. But he was not asleep or even at peace. How could he be when the raised voices of his twin grandsons could be heard all over the compound? Kamau sighed at the sound which disturbed him even more than the insects which kept trying to settle on his head and shoulders. At least he could drive these away with his horsehair fly swat.

It should have been peaceful in the compound, for the women and old folk were inside their huts and the young men had gone hunting. But it was not, for Mwangi and Njoroge were arguing as usual.

'You should help me move the cattle!' shouted Mwangi.

'I'm busy!' Njoroge shouted back, as he went on chasing his hoop.

'If you help me with the cattle now, I'll help you with the milking tomorrow morning,' Mwangi called out after him.

'Huh!' snorted Njoroge. 'You and your promises! Even if I helped you with the cattle, you'd find a way of getting out of helping me with the milking.'

'I would not!'

'Would!'

'Wouldn't!'

The argument continued until Mwangi saw that he was getting nowhere and began, noisily and grumpily, to get on with his job. With a great deal of shouting and whistling, he drove the cattle into their new enclosure. Then he returned to the compound feeling very hot and tired. The sight of Njoroge coolly continuing with his game of hoop-stick was the last straw. Mwangi rushed over to him and kicked the hoop with all his might. It went spinning madly away and

37

Njoroge shouted and lashed out angrily at his brother. Soon blows and insults were flying to and fro between the two boys.

At this, the twins' mother rushed out of her hut to pull the boys apart, box their ears and give them a good scolding. As she stalked back to her hut, she called out to them, 'One more quarrel from you and your father will hear about it!' Silenced at last, the boys stood and glared furiously at one another.

Having heard and seen everything, Kamau now called, 'Come, Njoroge! Come, Mwangi! I have a story for you.'

The boys turned and walked slowly across to the tree, their faces still angry and sullen. Njoroge flung himself down beside the old man's stool and began to draw pictures in the dust with one fast and furious forefinger while Mwangi sat hugging his knees.

Kamau spoke in his quiet old-man's voice.

'Once there was an old man who had seven sons. They should have been his pride and joy. But they were not. And why? Because they quarrelled and fought all the time, giving their father no peace.' At his feet Njoroge's dust-drawing became even more feverish and

Mwangi tightened his grip on his legs and pressed his face against them.

'One day,' Kamau continued, 'the old man asked his sons to gather round for he had something to show them. So they sat around their father, wondering what he would show them. But all he had in his hand were seven sticks. As the boys watched, their father tied these firmly together. Then he handed the bundle to his oldest son and said, "Try and break that."

'The oldest son strained with all his might to try and break the sticks. But he couldn't break even a single one. The same thing happened as each of the other brothers was handed the bundle and asked to do the same thing. The bundle could not be broken and each stick remained intact within it.

'Then the father untied the bundle and handed one of the sticks to his oldest son. "Now try and break that," he said. The oldest son took the stick and broke it easily. The same thing happened as each of the other brothers was handed one of the other sticks and asked to do the same thing. By the end, every stick had been broken.

'The old man paused before continuing, "Now do you understand what I have shown you? You could not break the sticks when they were tied together, for then they were strong. But how easily you broke them when they were separated, for then they were weak." '

Kamau stopped speaking for a moment. He stretched out his arms and gently laid a hand on the head of each of his silent grandsons.

'Njoroge, Mwangi,' he said, 'it is the same with people as with sticks. Our village is strong for we all work together and live in peace. If we were to fight and quarrel among ourselves, how easily would our enemies defeat us!'

Kamau put his hands back in his lap and closed his eyes. When he spoke again his voice was almost a whisper.

'This old one has told you the tale of another old one. You may find wisdom in it, if you wish. Now go, sons of my son, for I am very tired.'

The boys stood up, their faces no longer angry and sullen but ashamed and thoughtful. Then they walked quietly away, leaving their wise old grandfather to fall peacefully asleep on his three-legged stool in the shade of the spreading mugumo tree.

'Sonnet'

CATHERINE RICHARDS (AGED 16)

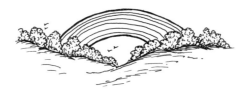

Come rain and wash the sins of man from earth
With soft sweet water falling from the skies,
Your droplets have caressed our cheeks since birth
And mingled with the tears that flow from eyes.
Now purge this land of all our evil deeds.
Drive out the hate and anger from within.
With tender love awake the sleeping seeds
And so command a new life to begin.

As humans we presume we own the world,
We fight, and wound and murder fellow men,
And even when the mercenaries grow old,
A younger generation start again.
So come now, rain, and with your soothing touch
Restore to us the love we need so much.

A Drop of Water

FAY SAMPSON

Phoebe bent over her baby brother. Kafulu's eyes were shut. His little
mouth gasped. She picked up a feeding-bottle and held it to his lips.
He sucked the water thirstily. She fed him a few drops more. Kafulu
was too weak with fever to drink for long. His head fell back across
Granny's knees.

'Will he die?' she asked.

'Who can say? We shall know more tomorrow when the nurse
comes.'

Tomorrow. The nurse would come on her bicycle, bringing her bag
of medicines and her thermometer. She would set up her clinic under
the shade tree in the middle of the village. She would know what to do.

If only Kafulu could last that long. He had a tummy illness.
His little body often needed washing. Milk made him sick. They fed
him water, mixed with salt and sugar.

'Phoebe! Hurry up, or it will be dinner-time before we get back
from the river. And there's a day's hoeing to be done.'

Her mother was calling. Usually Kafulu went everywhere with
Mama, strapped in a cloth on her back. But today he was too ill to be
carried, even in the early morning, when the shadows were cool. He
must stay with Granny. Her legs were too old and crippled to walk
the two miles to the river.

'Go quickly,' said Granny. 'The water is almost finished.'

Phoebe picked up the shiny jerrycan. She realized with a start that
it was empty. The bottle beside Kafulu was all that was left.

She ran out into the sunshine, lifting the jerrycan on to her head.
It hardly weighed anything when it was empty. But even when she
ran it didn't fall off her curly hair. Phoebe knew how to hold her
head high and steady.

The boys were playing football as she ran past. They never went to
fetch water. That was women's work. Phoebe saw the ball coming

41

her way. She kicked it back to the boys. Even then the jerrycan didn't wobble.

All the women and girls were filing into a narrow path that led out of the village. Grass grew shoulder-high on either side. Over the tops of the grass swayed a line of water-cans. Plastic and metal. Red, blue, gold, silver, as bright as humming-birds.

Phoebe fell in behind them, matching her mother's swinging stride. They began to sing.

As they walked along, other women joined them. They called, 'Good morning!'

'I hear your son Simon is coming home.'

'Isn't it wonderful! We haven't seen him for a year.'

A little further on,

'Rachel has had her baby – a fine big girl.'

'So you are a grandmother now. Congratulations!'

The path dipped. The trees became bigger, greener. The sand was growing damp under Phoebe's toes.

She saw the pool first. Brown water surrounded by reeds. A tiny river trickled in at one end and drained out at the other.

The women waded into the water. They washed the dust from their legs and splashed their hot faces. Some had brought clothes to wash.

Phoebe went in up to her knees. The muddy water was warm already. Her mother joked that there were crocodiles in the pool. Phoebe didn't believe her. But she was still careful.

Across the river was another village. More women came down the opposite bank to fetch their water. Morning and evening the two sides met here. The air rang with gossip and laughter.

Something splashed Phoebe's face. In front of her was Mpela, her friend from the other side, teasing her.

Then Mpela cried, 'Goats! They're dirtying our drinking water!'

At the head of the pool the river ran down over rocks in a clear waterfall. The girls raced towards it and chased the goats away.

'Phoebe! Have you filled your water-can? We must get back to Kafulu.'

Kafulu! How could she have forgotten her baby brother? Women were still waiting their turn for water. But they had heard about Kafulu. They stood back to let Phoebe go first, relaxing their strong shoulders.

'Go on. You have a sick baby.'

Mpela's mother laughed. 'Often I think it's this water that makes them sick.'

The water gushed into Phoebe's can. She quickly pushed the cap on and overtook Mama. Now she could only think about Kafulu. She ran on up the sandy path.

It was hot running uphill in the sunshine. The can was heavy now. But she could not wait to get home with the precious water.

She was far ahead of Mama, almost home. Something shot across the path, in front of Phoebe's bare toes. A black snake. She screamed and jumped back. The can of water on her head began to fall. The cap sprang off. Water splashed down into the dust.

The snake vanished. The can was steady between Phoebe's hands again. But for a long time she could not steady the beating of her heart. Suppose she had dropped it. Suppose she had lost a whole can of water.

She went on carefully now. The boys started weeding when they saw her coming. Phoebe walked past with her head held high, like a grown-up woman.

'Kafulu's asleep,' whispered Granny inside the dark hut.

The bottle was empty. Phoebe unscrewed the cap from her full can. She cleaned the bottle and boiled a little water. Kafulu's dry lips sucked. Then he opened his big brown eyes and smiled a thank-you.

Sam and the Hacker

From *Here I Am*

RUSSELL STANNARD

Here I Am is a book of imaginary conversations between a young computer buff, Sam, and God. God is 'the hacker', talking to Sam through his computer. Sam comes right back with a question.

'What are you doing these days – now that you're unemployed? Signing on at the Job Centre?'

'What? Sorry… I didn't get that…'

'Well, you created everything – got all this Universe going, right? So that's it. It just runs itself now. You aren't needed anymore.'

'Not needed! You don't create a world and then just go on holiday! Who do you think stops the Universe from disappearing? Who keeps it in existence?

'Look, Sam,' said the hacker. 'I am into everything that exists. It's a bit like being an author. An author doesn't just write the first sentence of the story and then leave the rest to write itself…'

'Hold on. A story? What are you saying now? I'm just a character in a story – a story you've made up. Is that it?'

'In a way, yes. In good stories the characters come alive; they take on a life of their own. The author starts off thinking he'll make them do this, or do that – but then he realizes such a person wouldn't do anything of the sort; they just wouldn't. So he has to give way; he has to write it differently. What comes out is a funny kind of mixture: what the author puts into it, but also what comes out of the characters themselves. Some characters are more famous than their authors. I enjoy being a character…'

'You? A character? But you just said you were the author. You can't be…'

'I'm both. I'm the Author of the story, but I'm also a character in the story. It's a story about me – living alongside people, working with them, sharing their troubles and joys…'

3

The Gift of Life

What is it that makes an oak tree grow,
or a little black rabbit so wonderfully alive?
What is the secret of life?
We know that living things need light and water.
There's quite a lot about that in these stories. But life itself
is something more. It's a great adventure. And if you find that
just a bit scary, *The Really Reluctant Raindrop* is the story for you.

'The Oak'

STUART LITTLE (AGED 14 YEARS)

Acorn
tiny, hidden
living, germinating, growing
shoots, roots – trunk, branches
swaying, blossoming, towering
sturdy, mighty
Oak

Big Tree, Little Tree

SYLVIA MANDEVILLE

'We learned a new song in school today,' said Daren to his Mum as he ate his tea. 'One about God making the sky and the trees. But it's not really true, is it,' he said, 'that bit about God making the trees?'

He looked down, out of the window, to the windswept courtyard far below, then beyond the flats to the park.

'When did he make that tree – that big one in the middle of the park?' he asked.

'That old oak tree?' said Mum. 'I should think he's been slowly making that tree for about two hundred years. Oak trees are slow growers.'

'Two hundred years!' exclaimed Daren. 'That's older than you and Dad, isn't it?' he said.

'Just a bit,' said Mum.

'But how did God start making the tree?' asked Daren. 'Did people just wake up one day, and there it was?'

'You go and find me your anorak, and I'll show you how God started to make that oak tree,' said Mum.

'My anorak?' said Daren.

'Yes,' said Mum.

Looking puzzled, Daren hunted for his anorak.

'Now turn out the pockets, and show me what you've got,' said Mum.

'Two marbles, a dirty hanky, a bus ticket, a bit of chewed gum and an acorn,' said Daren.

'Ah! It's the acorn I want,' said Mum. 'I saw you pick it up the other day in the park. Now that's what God starts with when he begins to make an oak tree.'

Daren looked at the dull brown acorn in surprise.

'An oak tree starts with an acorn?' he said. 'How?'

'We can watch and find out – but God works very slowly

sometimes, so you will have to be patient.' Mum went to the cupboard and hunted for a while. 'Here, this will do,' she said.

It was a small bottle. 'Fill it with water, please, Daren.'

When Daren had filled it with water, Mum put the acorn in at the top of the bottle. The tip of the acorn was just touching the water.

'Now put it on the window-sill, and we'll look at it every day and see what happens,' she said.

That night, when Dad came home from work, Daren told him about the acorn.

'We're going to watch God make an oak tree,' Daren said.

'You'll be an old man before it's finished,' Dad laughed. But when he said prayers with Daren that night he said, 'Please God, help Daren's acorn grow into a big oak tree.'

Next morning, Daren jumped out of bed and ran to the window-sill.

'Nothing's happened, Mum!' he called out. 'God hasn't made an oak tree like you said he would.'

'We told you you would have to be patient,' Dad called back.

Every day Daren looked at the acorn. At last one morning he called out excitedly.

'Hey! Mum! Look, it's begun to grow!' From the bottom of the acorn, a small shoot had sprouted.

'That is the first root growing,' said Mum. 'It is very strong. You see – it will fill the bottle before long.'

Every day the root had grown a little longer. It had to curl round to fit in the bottle. But no leaves grew at the top and no branch showed there.

'That takes a little longer to come,' said Dad. 'But if you lift the acorn gently from the bottle, you will see that something is happening.'

Daren lifted up the acorn. He was careful not to break the curly root. The brown skin was cracking off the acorn. Under the skin, the acorn was turning from cream to bright scarlet. It was also beginning to split at the bottom, and a tiny new shoot was showing.

'That is the stem coming,' said Mum. 'One day it will be a thick tree trunk.'

Several weeks later, the tiny shoot had grown upwards into a thin stem, as tall as Daren's hand. At the top were two bronze-coloured leaves.

'Now you can begin to see it looking really like an oak tree,' said Mum.

Daren looked across to the great oak in the park. Could his little tree really grow as big as that?

'What shall we do with our tree now?' he said. 'The root has filled the bottle and needs more room. Soon it will be so tall, it will topple over.'

'Why not ask your friend Carly if we can plant it in her garden? She doesn't live in a flat like us.'

Carly was very excited at the idea of planting an oak tree in her garden. Her Mum said it had better go in the corner, where the dog wouldn't dig it up.

'It's very tiny,' said Carly. 'Is it really an oak tree?'

'Yes,' said Daren. 'God's going to take hundreds of years to make it grow into a really big one.'

'When it's bigger we can climb in it and build a tree house,' said Carly.

'Yes!' said Daren.

Carly's Mum and Daren's Mum smiled at each other.

'Thoughts of a Seed'

BEN THACKERAY, ANDREW PIMBLOTT, PAUL ARMSTRONG, LAUREN EVES,
ROGER TWISS, DAVID CROSS AND RICHARD JONES (AGED 4–5)

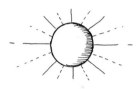

A little boy planted me;
   I feel cool and safe in the soil
   As black as dark.
   I'm thirsty now.
   Who will give me a drink?
   Here comes the rain.
When I push through the soil
   It will be hard,
As hard as a bone.
   I want to grow
   Into a sunflower, yellow bright.
   I want to grow
   Up, as high as the clouds.
Then the wind can blow
   And bend me;
My seeds will scatter
   And the little boy can eat them.
   They tell me I need light to grow.
I hope nobody switches off the light.

The Rain

A Story from East Africa

JENNY ROBERTSON

A boy called Tapi walked barefoot across the hard brown earth towards an old man sitting in the shade of a thorn bush. The old man had lived in the village for so long that everyone called him Grandfather.

'Hello, Grandfather,' called Tapi.

'Come and sit beside me, Tapi,' invited Grandfather. So Tapi sat down. His shadow disappeared into the shadow of the thorn bush.

'I'm so thirsty!' Tapi sighed.

'So am I,' said Grandfather. 'The whole land needs rain.'

'I've never seen rain,' said Tapi. 'Not that I can remember,' he added. 'But I know it comes from the clouds.'

He looked up at the sky. It was so blue it hurt his eyes.

'There are no clouds there,' he said.

A herd boy led thin cows by. He stopped beside Grandfather. 'When will the rain come?' he asked. 'Without rain no grass grows and the cows don't give milk. The cows are thirsty, and so am I.'

'And so am I!' said Tapi.

'Everyone is thirsty,' Grandfather said.

'I can see a cloud, Grandfather!' exclaimed Tapi. 'But it's a very small one.'

'One small cloud may bring others,' Grandfather explained.

'Let's go home now,' said Tapi.

They left the shade of the thorn bush and walked along slowly, dodging bare white bones across the path.

'The water-hole has dried up,' said Grandfather. 'Even if the rain comes soon it will be too late for some of the animals.'

'There's another cloud, Grandfather, and it's just a bit bigger.'

Grandfather rocked on his thin legs. His wrinkled eyelids closed. 'Tapi, Tapi, maybe the rain is on its way,' he whispered.

But by the time they reached the village the clouds had disappeared.

'The sky's so blue,' said Tapi. 'I think it must be thirsty too, Grandfather.'

Tapi's mother greeted Grandfather. Her baby was asleep on her back. His cheek rested against her shoulder as she tipped out the last kernels of grain from a flat basket. 'My baby cried himself to sleep,' she said. 'The land is crying for rain like my baby.'

'We have heard the cries, Tapi and I,' said Grandfather.

His mother fetched the water jar. 'There's just a mouthful left,' she said, offering the jar to Grandfather. Tapi waited, swallowing hard. Grandfather barely moistened his lips with the water, and handed the jar to Tapi.

'Look, Tapi, the clouds have come back,' he said.

'There are more this time,' Tapi counted.

And all afternoon they watched the sky grow dark with clouds until there were too many to count.

'Go and lie down, Tapi,' said Grandfather. 'Perhaps the rain will come while we're asleep.'

Grandfather was right. The rain came that night. Tapi woke to hear it drumming on their roof. He opened his eyes. His father stood beside him. 'It's raining,' his father said.

Tapi jumped up and raced outside. Rain rushed over their sloping roof. He was drenched immediately. He bumped into his mother. She was putting out all the water jars to catch the rain.

The whole village must have got up. Hens flapped their wings and scurried, squawking from the downpour, but everyone else was outside, filling jars and containers with the rain. Tapi gasped as raindrops stung his eyes. He tasted them in his open mouth. A hand touched his shoulder. 'How do you like the rain?' asked Grandfather.

'It's good.' Tapi nodded.

The dry earth sucked up the rain. A good moist smell rose from the ground. Cows mooed. The water-holes filled and rivers flowed. All the animals crowded round to drink.

Everyone carried their water jars into their homes and went back to sleep feeling very happy.

'The Tyger'

WILLIAM BLAKE

Tyger! Tyger! burning bright
In the forests of the night,
What immortal hand or eye
Could frame thy fearful symmetry?

In what distant deeps or skies
Burnt the fire of thine eyes?
On what wings dare he aspire?
What the hand dare seize the fire?

And what shoulder, & what art,
Could twist the sinews of thy heart?
And when thy heart began to beat,
What dread hand? & what dread feet?

What the hammer? what the chain?
In what furnace was thy brain?
What the anvil? what dread grasp
Dare its deadly terrors clasp?

When the stars threw down their spears,
And water'd heaven with their tears,
Did he smile his work to see?
Did he who made the Lamb make thee?

Tyger! Tyger! burning bright
In the forests of the night,
What immortal hand or eye,
Dare frame thy fearful symmetry?

The Little Black Rabbit

From *Shadrach*

MEINDERT DEJONG

There was this boy, Davie, and he was going to have a rabbit. His grandfather had promised it. A real, live rabbit! A little black rabbit, if possible. In a week, if possible.

There was this boy, Davie, and he was going to have a rabbit in a week. And here he was, in his grandfather's barn on the first long afternoon of that long waiting week. He was lying in front of the empty rabbit hutch. He was peering into the hutch. He had a whole long week to wait for his rabbit, but he already had the hutch. His father had made it for him.

It was the longest week of Davie's life, waiting for Maartens' wagon to bring him the rabbit. Then, at last…

'Mum, Mum,' he yelled. 'Maartens is coming down the road. Maartens is coming!' He dashed on again, on to Grandpa's.

He was far down the street when his mother called from the door: 'Davie, Davie, not so fast, not so hard! Davie, your umbrella!'

He made believe he did not hear, and raced on.

Grandfather wasn't in the barn. He stormed into the house. Grandpa and Grandma were eating. It brought him up short, he hadn't expected that. Now he couldn't ask Grandpa to go out to Maartens' wagon with him, not when Grandpa was eating.

'Grandpa,' he panted. 'Maartens is coming! He'll soon be in the village, he's just stopping at those three houses out on that side road, and then he'll be here. And it's raining hard. Oh, Grandpa!'

Grandpa tried to calm him. 'Look, Davie. Maartens has to make many a stop at the outlying houses before he gets into the village, so there's plenty of time. Suppose you just sit nicely down with us to eat. Oh, that herring's good!'

'I can't eat,' he said impatiently. 'And Mother says I shouldn't eat when I'm so excited.'

'Oh,' Grandpa grunted. 'Well, may I eat, Davie? There's really plenty of time.'

Grandma shook her head.

He couldn't even stand the smell of the herring. He looked anxiously out of the window, although that window didn't look out on the road at all. 'I'm going quick to put some fresh food in the crib for when he comes,' he suddenly decided aloud. He had to do something.

'I think that's the best idea yet,' Grandpa said. 'We've got to have everything ready.'

He dashed to the barn, but there he stood. There was plenty of fresh food in the little crib. There was nothing to do. Time stood still. It was awful.

He peered out at the pouring rain. Maartens would stop at all the outlying houses before coming into the village – stand there in the rain waiting at each house... He could stand the waiting no longer. Waiting was just like pain. It hurt. He wished he hadn't thrown the umbrella into Mother's hall. If he had the umbrella, he could go out to look for the wagon, follow it even... But the way it was pouring now he knew that if he went home, Mother wouldn't let him go out again. He thought of something. Grandpa always pulled a sack over his head and shoulders when he got caught in the rain on his farm. He grabbed a sack and draped it over his head and shoulders. Then he dashed.

He ran hard all the way out of the village, all the way to the little side road. Just as he reached it, there Maartens' old horse came turning out of it. Now the wagon was coming towards him. All of a sudden there they were. He stood at the side of the road, the words all ready in his mouth to say to Maartens, 'Hello, Maartens. Maartens, have you got my little rabbit?'

The wagon passed him so close, the hub of the front wheel almost grazed him. But Maartens became busy ringing a bell to announce to the village that he was coming. Maartens didn't even see him. Maartens looked cross and wet and angry, and everything dripped with rain. The words had been ready in his mouth, but all of a sudden he went shy and couldn't think of them. When he thought of them, the wagon was past.

Dumbly, miserably he started to follow the wagon. There was nobody in the streets, just the old wagon in the rain, just he behind the wagon, walking under his sack. Nobody stopped the wagon. Now and then a woman took the trouble to open the door a moment, and shout: 'Nothing today, Maartens.' Up at the front on the high seat he could hear Maartens muttering to himself in the rain. The old wagon lumbered on again, and he followed. Now the rain really poured down.

Then just as Maartens was beginning the turn into a side street, a woman's voice came through the rain, a woman was talking to Maartens. Was that Mother? The wagon had stopped, but the rain drummed so hard on the canvas, he couldn't be sure he had heard right. He scrunched down, carefully peered through the spokes of a wheel. It *was* Mother! Mother had stopped Maartens! She had Grandpa's big umbrella. She hadn't waited for Maartens to come to their house... But what if she caught him here in the rain, all soaked?

'Maartens, did you bring the rabbit we wrote about?'

He had heard it plainly. Mother was shouting against the drum of the rain on the canvas.

He stood deathly still. It had never crossed his mind – that he had never thought of – that there might be no rabbit. He waited without a breath in his body, straining to hear what Maartens would say. The rain drummed. He hurriedly sneaked along the far side of the wagon to hear what Maartens would say.

'Now let me see, let me see,' Maartens was rumbling. 'Did I put that rabbit on this morning, or didn't I?'

It was unbelievable – unimaginable – Maartens not knowing that!

Now Maartens was rummaging about in the wagon to see if he had brought the rabbit. It couldn't be believed!

At last Maartens spoke up. 'Yup, got him. There he is all safe and snug. Tucked him so far down under the straw and stuff, I clean forgot I had him. Ho ho ho, that's a good one.'

'Oh!' He felt limp.

'Thank goodness,' Mother was saying. 'I don't know what would have happened if there hadn't been a rabbit. It's black, I hope?'

'Black as sin,' Maartens said. 'You wouldn't be interested in some nice cups and saucers? Just got them in from England.'

Now they were talking about dishes, not even bothering about the little rabbit. He could hold out no longer. He hurled himself around the wagon and the patient old horse. 'Mother, make him give it to me,' he yelled.

His mother whirled.

'Make him hand the rabbit down!'

'Davie! What are you doing here in all the rain? Look at you soaked! And that dirty, wet sack!'

He didn't care about any of it. 'Make him give it to me.'

'I ought to make him take it back! Look at you.'

He didn't for a moment consider the threat.

Maartens was leaning down from the seat. 'So, is that your boy? Why, he's been following the wagon all through the village. I was wondering what ailed the little fellow, but I never thought of the rabbit.'

Now they were talking! He couldn't stand it. He tried to clamber up the spokes of the wagon to get at Maartens and the little rabbit. And now at last Maartens reached behind the seat and pulled up a little wooden box and held it down to him. There was his rabbit! He grabbed the box. It had little air holes. It was too dark. He started off with the box, turned back. 'Mother, I can't see him. And it's raining, and he'll get all wet. I've got to get to Grandpa's barn. Mother!'

'Oh,' she said, 'so now you're worried about the rabbit getting wet!' She still had to tell Maartens a few quick last things, but then she came. She held the umbrella over him. Together they half galloped down the rainy street under the big black umbrella. He hugged the box to his chest. 'Oh, Mother.'

'Yes – oh, Mother – but you're soaked and cold and chilled, and the moment you get your rabbit in that hutch, you're going straight to bed.'

He knew it for the hollow threat it was, he didn't even listen to it. 'Mum, Grandpa and Grandma will be sitting there eating, and all the time we'll have the little rabbit in the hutch, and then we'll tell Grandpa. You know what? We'll tell him there's some animal in the barn. A rat! And there he'll come, maybe with a club, even. And all the time it will be my little black rabbit, and then he'll see it… Mum, you can't run very fast, can you? Oh, Mum, I've got my little rabbit. And Mum, you went after him too.'

'Yes,' Mother said. 'I wanted to surprise you. I just wanted to see your face.'

'Oh, Mum,' he said, and it had to express all his great gratitude and all his excitement. 'Mum, can't we go faster?'

At last they were there. And Mother had the top of the hutch open, and he had his hand down in the dark box, and in his hand was something silky, furry, and warm. It moved – *it lived*! Soft and warm and it lived! Gently, a little fearfully, he lowered the little black furry handful into the hutch, scared and careful not to clutch too hard, and afraid at the same time the little rabbit might wriggle free and fall to the ground and hurt himself.

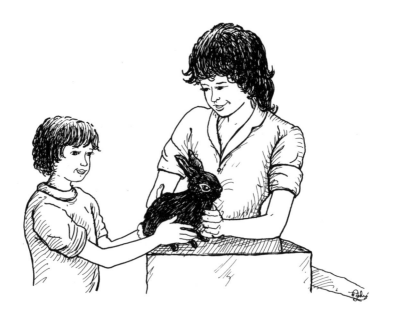

There he was – there sat the little furry ball, black on the gleaming yellow straw. There he was in the hutch. Shadrach! He wanted badly to take him out again, didn't dare take him out again – no, he was safer in the hutch. But for a moment he had held him, felt him – alive!

The Really Reluctant Raindrop

JEAN WATSON

Dorp was a really reluctant raindrop. He did not want to leave his cloudy nest high up in the sky. Not one bit.

'I want to stay here for ever,' he said.

'Don't be such a drip,' said the other raindrops. 'Besides, you can't stay here for much longer. We're all getting fatter by the minute and soon we'll fall.'

'Don't drop me, cloud! Please don't drop me!' pleaded Dorp.

'But I must,' said the cloud softly. 'I cannot hold you much longer. Soon you will begin your first adventure.'

'But I don't want adventures. Heeeelp!' cried Dorp, beginning to drop.

Leaving the cloud, he fell faster and faster, through the air towards the misty-coloured mountain peaks.

'Oh, dear! Oh, dear!' cried Dorp. 'This will be my downfall.'

'Ha, ha! That's very good,' said another falling raindrop. 'Quite a comic, aren't you?'

'Me – a comic?' shrieked Dorp. 'You must be joking!'

'I thought that's what *you* were doing,' laughed the other, before being swept away on a gust of wind.

'Oh, dear! Oh, dear!' quavered Dorp, 'I'm petrified.'

'Liquefied, actually,' said a different raindrop, falling close by. 'And my advice to you is – stop worrying. It'll be all right. This is my third adventure, so I should know.'

'But where are we all going? What will become of me?' asked Dorp.

'I cannot answer your questions,' was the reply. 'Every adventure is different and your first one is coming up right now.'

The ground was now only a few feet away and Dorp closed his eyes and waited for the bump but it never came. Instead he landed, painlessly, in some water to be swept down a steep slope. On either side goats were grazing.

'Where am I?' gasped Dorp.

'In a stream, brook, rivulet, gully, beck – take your pick,' was the babbling reply. 'What's in a name, anyway? It's what you *do* that matters. And what *I* do is splash, swish, gurgle, splutter, spurt down to the river.'

'Oh, dear! Oh, dear!' moaned Dorp. 'But I don't want to go to the river.'

'Not want to go to the river?' bubbled the stream. 'Not want to join the great, deep, swelling water as it snakes, surges and sweeps across the land? Well, words fail me.' (Which they didn't – not for long, anyway.)

'But rivers are so… big,' protested fearful Dorp.

'Big is not always bad, terrible, alarming,' tinkled the stream. 'Sometimes big is beautiful, breathtaking, inspiring. Just let yourself *go.*'

So Dorp tried to let himself go. And, after a time, he found that it was not so bad to be rushing down a mountain between heather-covered slopes. And, after a bit more time, he said, 'If I can't be back in my cloud, I'd like to stay here for ever and ever.'

The stream laughed, not unkindly, and rippled, 'No way can a little raindrop swim against the current, tide, flow. You'll have to take what comes. And what comes now is the river – glump!'

At first Dorp was panic-stricken at being swept into the wide waters. But then he realized that he was floating, quite safely and slowly, between grassy banks.

'So this is the river,' he murmured.

'The river, the river,' answered a deep, slow, echoing voice.

'Where are you taking me?' asked Dorp.

'No patience, no trust!' said the voice. 'Always afraid of the next thing. Never happy *now.*'

'I'm sorry,' said Dorp. 'But perhaps if I knew what was *going to* happen, I would be able to enjoy what's happening *now.*'

'I doubt it,' said the river. 'If I were to tell you what the future held, you'd get frightened about that, or something else.'

'I don't *want* to be frightened,' said Dorp.

'That's a good start, a good start,' was the answer. 'So think about what's happening to you right now. Look around. What could be nicer than cruising along with plenty to see and hear? Just let yourself *be.*'

So Dorp tried to let himself be. And, after a time, he found that it was not so bad to be winding past fields and tickled by trout. And, after a bit more time, he said, 'If I can't be back in my cloud or in the stream, I'd like to stay here for ever and ever.'

'Cannot be done, cannot be done,' replied the river. 'Sooner or later – and in your case, sooner – you will join the sea.'

'But the sea is so... huge and wide and deep and fierce,' protested Dorp.

'And magnificent and wise and full of wonders,' added the river but the raindrop was listening to the roaring of the sea, which grew louder and louder until, almost deafened, he was swept into its cold, salty waves.

At first the noise and movement was too much for him, but then he realized that he was quite safe and was getting used to the noise.

'How long will I be here?' he whispered.

'Who knows?' replied the sea, in a voice like thunder. 'The sun and moon and wind are my masters and yours, too. You may be with me for a long time, or gone with the wind tomorrow. Who knows? Just let yourself *live*.'

So Dorp tried to let himself live. And, after a time, he found that it was not so bad to ride up and down the waves and be part of the strange and beautiful world of the sea. And, after a bit more time, he said, 'If I can't be in my cloud or in the stream or river, I'd like to stay here for ever and ever.'

But even as he spoke, he was sucked into the air.

'Oh, dear! Oh, dear! Where am I going now?' he cried, feeling strangely light and dry. But the wind made no answer as it swept him up, then across the sea and over the land.

At first Dorp shivered and shook with fear. But then he seemed to hear three voices, blown on the wind. The first one babbled, 'Let yourself go.' The second urged, 'Let yourself be.' And the third thundered, 'Let yourself live.'

Dorp tried to let himself go, be and live. And, after a time, he found that it was not so bad to be sweeping across the land – until he saw mountain peaks ahead and started quivering again. But the wind lifted him high into the cold air, way, way above the mountain tops.

Then, suddenly, Dorp found himself back in his cloudy nest.

'Home! Home at last!' he exclaimed happily.

But he kept thinking and thinking about the stream and the river, the sea and the wide, wonderful world. And the longing to see them again grew stronger and stronger, until one day he surprised himself by saying, 'I think I'm ready for my second adventure.'

But the cloud didn't seem at all surprised. She smiled and said, 'You don't seem a bit like the shivering, shaking, really reluctant raindrop you used to be.'

'What a wimp!' exclaimed Dorp pulling a face. Then he smiled. 'That was then,' he said. 'And this,' he shouted as he dive-bombed straight through the cloud, 'is now. Whooppeeee!'

4

What a Wonderful World!

The stories and poems in this section celebrate the world of nature – the unique beauty of a snowflake, Mole and Ratty's chuckling river, the waves crashing on the shore at high tide. There is something here for everyone.
Do you find wild animals 'awesome'? What do you think about toads? Do you love the night, or are you scared of the dark, like the boy in *Switch on the Night*? And how about living in the wild, as Sam Gribley does in *Winter and Summer*?

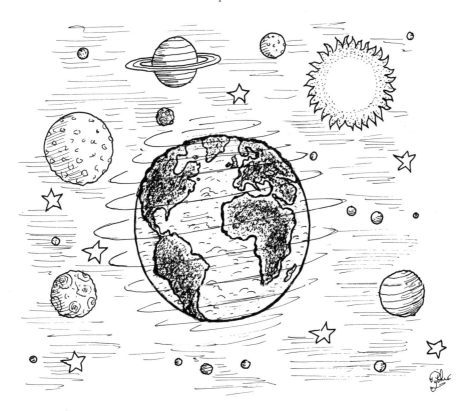

'The World'

WILLIAM BRIGHTY RANDS

Great, wide, beautiful, wonderful World,
With the wonderful water round you curled,
And the wonderful grass upon your breast –
World, you are beautifully dressed.

The wonderful air is over me,
And the wonderful wind is shaking the tree,
It walks on the water, and whirls the mills,
And talks to itself on the tops of the hills.

You friendly Earth, how far do you go,
With the wheatfields that nod and the rivers that flow,
With cities and gardens, and cliffs, and isles,
And people upon you for thousands of miles?

Ah, you are so great, and I am so small,
I tremble to think of you, World at all;
And yet, when I said my prayers today,
A whisper inside me seemed to say,
'You are more than the Earth, though you are such a dot;
You can love and think and the Earth cannot'.

The Black Fox

From *The Midnight Fox*

BETSY BYARS

I did not believe it for a minute. It was like my eyes were playing a trick or something, because I was just sort of staring across this field, thinking about my letter, and then in the distance, where the grass was very green, I saw a fox leaping over the crest of the field. The grass moved and the fox sprang towards the movement, and then, seeing that it was just the wind that had caused the grass to move, she ran straight for the grove of trees where I was sitting.

It was so great that I wanted it to start over again, like you can turn movie film back and see yourself repeat some fine thing you have done, and I wanted to see the fox leaping over the grass again. In all my life I have never been so excited.

I did not move at all, but I could hear the paper in my hand shaking, and my heart seemed to have moved up my body and got stuck in my throat.

The fox came straight towards the grove of trees. She wasn't afraid, and I knew she had not seen me against the tree. I stayed absolutely still even though I felt like jumping up and screaming, 'Aunt Millie! Uncle Fred! Come see this. It's a fox, *a fox*!'

Her steps as she crossed the field were lighter and quicker than a cat's. As she came closer I could see that her black fur was tipped with white. It was as if it were midnight and the moon were shining on her fur, frosting it. The wind parted her fur as it changed directions. Suddenly she stopped. She was ten feet away now, and with the changing of the wind she got my scent. She looked right at me.

I did not move for a moment and neither did she. Her head was cocked to one side, her tail curled up, her front left foot raised. In all my life I never saw anything like that fox standing there with her pale golden eyes on me and this great black fur being blown by the wind.

Suddenly her nose quivered. It was such a slight movement I almost didn't see it, and then her mouth opened and I could see the pink tip of her tongue. She turned. She still was not afraid, but with a bound that was lighter than the wind – it was as if she was being blown away over the field – she was gone.

Still I didn't move. I couldn't. I couldn't believe that I had really seen the fox.

I had seen foxes before in zoos, but I was always in such a great hurry to get on to the good stuff that I was saying stupid things like, 'I want to see the go-rilllllllas,' and not once had I ever really looked at a fox. Still, I could never remember seeing a black fox, not even in a zoo.

Also, there was a great deal of difference between seeing an animal in the zoo in front of painted fake rocks and trees and seeing one natural and free in the woods. It was like seeing a kite on the floor and then, later, seeing one up in the sky where it was supposed to be, pulling at the wind.

I started to pick up my pencil and write as quickly as I could, 'P.S. Today I saw a black fox.' But I didn't. This was the most exciting thing that had happened to me, and 'P.S. Today I saw a black fox' made it nothing. 'So what else is happening?' Petie Burkis would probably write back. I folded my letter, put it in an envelope, and sat there.

I thought about this old newspaper that my dad had had in his desk drawer for years. It was orange and the headline was just one word, very big, the letters about twelve inches high. WAR! And I mean it was awesome to see that word like that, because you knew it was a word that was going to change your whole life, the whole world even. And every time I would see that newspaper, even though I wasn't even born when it was printed, I couldn't say anything for a minute or two.

Well, this was the way I felt right then about the black fox. I thought about a newspaper with just one word for a headline, very big, very black letters, twelve inches high. FOX! And even that did not show how awesome it had really been to me.

'To a Snowflake'

FRANCIS THOMPSON

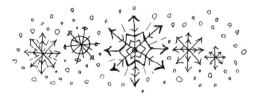

What heart could have thought you? –
Past our devisal
(O filigree petal!)
Fashioned so purely,
Fragilely, surely,
From what Paradisal
Imagineless metal,
Too costly for cost?
Who hammered you, wrought you,
From argentine vapour? –

'God was my Shaper.
Passing surmisal,
He hammered, he wrought me,
From curled silver vapour,
To lust of his mind: –
Thou couldst not have thought me!
So purely, so palely,
Tinily, surely,
Mightily, frailly,
Insculped and embossed,
With his hammer of wind,
And his graver of frost.'

Winter and Summer

From *My Side of the Mountain*

JEAN GEORGE

Sam Gribley has run away to the Catskill Mountains. He has left his parents, his eight brothers and sisters, and their cramped New York flat. He has a penknife, a ball of string, an axe and forty dollars. He is determined to survive in the wild.

'I am on my mountain in a tree home that people have passed without ever knowing that I am here. The house is a hemlock tree six feet in diameter, and must be as old as the mountain itself. I came upon it last summer and dug and burned it out until I made a snug cave in the tree that I now call home.

'My bed is on the right as you enter, and is made of ash slats and covered with deerskin. On the left is a small fireplace about knee high. It is of clay and stones. It has a chimney that leads the smoke out through a knothole. I chipped out three other knotholes to let fresh air in. The air coming in is bitter cold. It must be below zero outside, and yet I can sit here inside my tree and write with bare hands. The fire is small, too. It doesn't take much fire to warm this tree room.

'It is the fourth of December, I think. It may be the fifth. I am not sure because I have not recently counted the notches in the aspen pole that is my calendar. I have been just too busy gathering nuts and berries, smoking venison, fish, and small game to keep up with the exact date.

'The lamp I am writing by is deer fat poured into a turtle-shell with a strip of my old city trousers for a wick.

'It snowed all day yesterday and today. I have not been outside since the storm began, and I am bored for the first time since I ran away from home eight months ago to live on the land.

'I am well and healthy. The food is good. Sometimes I eat turtle soup, and I know how to make acorn pancakes. I keep my supplies in the wall of the tree in wooden pockets that I chopped myself.

'Every time I have looked at those pockets during the last two days, I have felt just like a squirrel, which reminds me: I didn't see a squirrel one whole day before that storm began. I guess they are holed up and eating their stored nuts, too.

'I wonder if The Baron, that's the wild weasel who lives behind the big boulder to the north of my tree, is also denned up. Well, anyway, I think the storm is dying down because the tree is not crying so much. When the wind really blows, the whole tree moans right down to the roots, which is where I am.

'Tomorrow I hope The Baron and I can tunnel out into the sunlight. I wonder if I should dig the snow. But that would mean I would have to put it somewhere, and the only place to put it is in my nice snug tree. Maybe I can pack it with my hands as I go. I've always dug into the snow from the top, never up from under.

'The Baron must dig up from under the snow. I wonder where he puts what he digs? Well, I guess I'll know in the morning.'

When I wrote that last winter, I was scared and thought maybe I'd never get out of my tree. I had been scared for two days – ever since the first blizzard hit the Catskill Mountains. When I came up to the sunlight, which I did by simply poking my head into the soft snow and standing up, I laughed at my dark fears.

Everything was white, clean, shining, and beautiful. The sky was blue, blue, blue. The hemlock grove was laced with snow, the meadow was smooth and white, and the gorge was sparkling with ice. It was so beautiful and peaceful that I laughed out loud. I guess I laughed because my first snowstorm was over and it had not been so terrible after all.

Then I shouted, 'I did it!' My voice never got very far. It was hushed by the tons of snow.

I looked for signs of The Baron Weasel. His footsteps were all over the boulder, also slides where he had played. He must have been up for hours, enjoying the new snow.

Inspired by his fun, I poked my head into my tree and whistled. Frightful, my trained falcon, flew to my fist, and we jumped and slid down the mountain, making big holes and trenches as we went. It was good to be whistling and carefree again, because I was sure scared by the coming of that storm.

I had been working since May, learning how to make a fire with flint and steel, finding what plants I could eat, how to trap animals and catch fish – all this so that when the curtain of blizzard struck the Catskills, I could crawl inside my tree and be comfortably warm and have plenty to eat.

During the summer and fall I had thought about the coming of winter. However, on that third day of December when the sky blackened, the temperature dropped, and the first flakes swirled around me, I must admit that I wanted to run back to New York. Even the first night that I spent out in the woods, when I couldn't get the fire started, was not as frightening as the snowstorm that gathered behind the gorge and mushroomed up over my mountain.

I was smoking three trout. It was nine o'clock in the morning. I was busy keeping the flames low so they would not leap up and burn the fish. As I worked, it occurred to me that it was awfully dark for that hour of the morning. Frightful was leashed to her tree stub. She seemed restless and pulled at her tethers. Then I realized that the forest was dead quiet. Even the woodpeckers that had been tapping around me all morning were silent. The squirrels were nowhere to be seen. The juncos and chickadees and nuthatches were gone. I looked to see what The Baron Weasel was doing. He was not around. I looked up.

From my tree you can see the gorge beyond the meadow. White water pours between the black wet boulders and cascades into the valley below. The water that day was as dark as the rocks. Only the sound told me it was still falling. Above the darkness stood another darkness. The clouds of winter, black and fearsome. They looked as wild as the winds that were bringing them. I grew sick with fright. I knew I had enough food. I knew everything was going to be perfectly all right. But knowing that didn't help. I was scared. I stamped out the fire, and pocketed the fish.

I tried to whistle for Frightful, but couldn't purse my shaking lips tight enough to get out anything but *pfffff*. So I grabbed her by the hide straps that are attached to her legs and we dove through the deerskin door into my room in the tree.

I put Frightful on the bedpost, and curled up in a ball on the bed. I thought about New York and the noise and the lights and how a snowstorm always seemed very friendly there. I thought about our apartment, too. At that moment it seemed bright and lighted and warm. I had to keep saying to myself: There were eleven of us in it!

70

Dad, Mother, four sisters, four brothers, and me. And not one of us liked it, except perhaps little Nina, who was too young to know. Dad didn't like it even a little bit. He had been a sailor once, but when I was born, he gave up the sea and worked on the docks in New York. Dad didn't like the land. He liked the sea, wet and big and endless.

Sometimes he would tell me about Great-grandfather Gribley, who owned land in the Catskill Mountains and felled the trees and built a home and ploughed the land – only to discover that he wanted to be a sailor. The farm failed, and Great-grandfather Gribley went to sea.

As I lay with my face buried in the sweet greasy smell of my deerskin, I could hear Dad's voice saying, 'That land is still in the family's name. Somewhere in the Catskills is an old beech with the name *Gribley* carved on it. It marks the northern boundary of Gribley's folly – the land is no place for a Gribley.'

'The land is no place for a Gribley,' I said. 'The land is no place for a Gribley, and here I am three hundred feet from the beech with *Gribley* carved on it.'

I fell asleep at that point, and when I awoke I was hungry. I cracked some walnuts, got down the acorn flour I had pounded, with a bit of ash to remove the bite, reached out of the door for a little snow, and stirred up some acorn pancakes. I cooked them on a top of a tin can, and as I ate them, smothered with blueberry jam, I knew that the land was just the place for a Gribley.

'I Like the World'

STEVE TURNER

I like the world
The world is good
World of water
World of wood
World of feather
World of bone
World of mountain
World of stone.

World of fibre
World of spark
World of sunshine
World of dark
World of raindrop
World of dew
World of me
and
World of you.

The River

From *The Wind in the Willows*

KENNETH GRAHAME

Never in his life had Mole seen a river before – this sleek, sinuous, full-bodied animal, chasing and chuckling, gripping things with a gurgle and leaving them with a laugh, to fling itself on fresh playmates that shook themselves free, and were caught and held again. All was a-shake and a-shiver – glints and gleams and sparkles, rustle and swirl, chatter and bubble. The Mole was bewitched, entranced, fascinated. By the side of the river he trotted as one trots, when very small, by the side of a man who holds one spellbound by exciting stories; and when tired at last, he sat on the bank, while the river still chattered on to him, a babbling procession of the best stories in the world, sent from the heart of the earth to be told at last to the insatiable sea.

As he sat on the grass and looked across the river, a dark hole in the bank opposite, just above the water's edge, caught his eye, and dreamily he fell to considering what a nice snug dwelling-place it would make for an animal with few wants and fond of a bijou riverside residence, above flood level and remote from noise and dust. As he gazed, something bright and small seemed to twinkle down in the heart of it, vanished, then twinkled once more like a tiny star. But it could hardly be a star in such an unlikely situation; and it was too glittering and small for a glow-worm.

Then, as he looked, it winked at him, and so declared itself to be an eye; and a small face began gradually to grow up round it, like a frame round a picture.

A brown little face, with whiskers.

A grave round face, with the same twinkle in its eye that had first attracted his notice.

Small neat ears and thick silky hair.

It was the Water Rat!

Then the two animals stood and regarded each other cautiously.

73

'Hullo, Mole!' said the Water Rat.

'Hullo, Rat!' said the Mole.

'Would you like to come over?' inquired the Rat presently.

'Oh, it's all very well to *talk*,' said the Mole, rather pettishly, he being new to a river and riverside life and its ways.

The Rat said nothing, but stooped and unfastened a rope and hauled on it; then lightly stepped into a little boat which the Mole had not observed. It was painted blue outside and white within, and was just the size for two animals; and the Mole's whole heart went out to it at once, even though he did not yet fully understand its uses.

The Rat sculled smartly across and made fast. Then he held up his fore-paw as the Mole stepped gingerly down. 'Lean on that!' he said. 'Now then, step lively!' and the Mole to his surprise and rapture found himself actually seated in the stern of a real boat.

'This has been a wonderful day!' said he, as the Rat shoved off and took to the sculls again. 'Do you know, I've never been in a boat before in all my life.'

'What?' cried the Rat, open-mouthed: 'Never been in a – you never – well, I – what have you been doing, then?'

'Is it so nice as all that?' asked the Mole shyly, though he was quite prepared to believe it as he leant back in his seat and surveyed the cushions, the oars, the rowlocks, and all the fascinating fittings, and felt the boat sway lightly under him.

'Nice? It's the *only* thing,' sad the Water Rat solemnly, as he leant forward for his stroke. 'Believe me, my young friend, there is *nothing* – absolutely nothing – half so much worth doing as simply messing about in boats. Simply messing,' he went on dreamily: 'messing – about – in – boats; messing – '

'Look ahead, Rat!' cried the Mole suddenly.

It was too late. The boat struck the bank full tilt. The dreamer, the joyous oarsman, lay on his back at the bottom of the boat, his heels in the air.

' – about in boats – or *with* boats,' the Rat went on composedly, picking himself up with a pleasant laugh. 'In or out of 'em, it doesn't matter. Nothing seems really to matter, that's the charm of it. Whether you get away, or whether you don't; whether you arrive at your destination or whether you reach somewhere else, or whether you never get anywhere at all, you're always busy and you never do anything in particular; and when you've done it there's always something else to do, and you can do it if you like, but you'd much better not. Look here! If you've really nothing else on hand this morning, supposing we drop down the river together, and have a long day of it?'

The Mole waggled his toes from sheer happiness, spread his chest with a sigh of full contentment, and leaned back blissfully into the soft cushions. '*What* a day I'm having!' he said. 'Let us start at once!'

'Hold hard a minute, then!' said the Rat. He looped the painter through a ring in his landing-stage, climbed up into his hole above, and after a short interval reappeared staggering under a fat, wicker luncheon-basket.

'Shove that under your feet,' he observed to the Mole, as he passed it down into the boat. Then he untied the painter and took the sculls again.

'What's inside it?' asked the Mole, wriggling with curiosity.

'There's cold chicken inside it,' replied the Rat briefly; 'coldtonguecoldhamcoldbeefpickledgherkinssaladfrenchrollscress-sandwidgespottedmeatgingerbeerlemonadesodawater – '

'O stop, stop,' cried the Mole in ecstasies: 'This is too much!'

'Do you really think so?' inquired the Rat seriously. 'It's only what

I always take on these little excursions; and the other animals are always telling me that I'm a mean beast and cut it *very* fine!'

The Mole never heard a word he was saying. Absorbed in the new life he was entering upon, intoxicated with the sparkle, the ripple, the scents and the sounds and the sunlight, he trailed a paw in the water and dreamed long waking dreams. The Water Rat, like the good little fellow he was, sculled steadily on and forebore to disturb him.

'I like your clothes awfully, old chap,' he remarked after some half an hour or so had passed. 'I'm going to get a black velvet smoking suit myself some day, as soon as I can afford it.'

'I beg your pardon,' said the Mole, pulling himself together with an effort. 'You must think me very rude; but all this is so new to me. So – this – is – a – River!'

'*The* River,' corrected the Rat.

'And you really live by the river? What a jolly life!'

'By it and with it and on it and in it,' said the Rat. 'It's brother and sister to me, and aunts, and company, and food and drink, and (naturally) washing. It's my world, and I don't want any other.'

'The Toad'

HELEN SOUTHWOOD (AGED 13)

He crouched
Stone-still,
Like a small speckled rock;
With pulsating throat,
He looked so helpless,
So terrified.

His strong legs
Were folded,
Like springs,
Held close.

Light as a leaf,
As big as my palm,
He sat in the scoop
Of my hands.

Now, his pads,
Like minute claws,
Cling for life.
His tiny toes
Clutch my fingertips.

His skin is lumpy,
Soft and bumpy,
His rough belly
Warming my palm.

So eager, so anxious
To run from me,
He does not know
I am harmless;
He is beautiful.
If only he knew!

The Key

From *The Secret Garden*

FRANCES HODGSON BURNETT

*When orphan Mary Lennox comes from India to Misselthwaite
Manor to live with her uncle, everybody says she is the most
disagreeable-looking child ever seen. She is rude and cross and
selfish. But Misselthwaite holds a secret, and Mary's discovery
will soon change everything, including herself.*

The flower-bed was not quite bare. It was bare of flowers because the
perennial plants had been cut down for their winter rest, but there
were tall shrubs and low ones which grew together at the back of the
bed, and as the robin hopped about under them, Mary saw him hop
over a small pile of freshly turned-up earth. He stopped on it to look
for a worm. The earth had been turned up because a dog had been
trying to dig up a mole and he had scratched quite a deep hole.

Mary looked at it, not really knowing why the hole was there, and
as she looked she saw something almost buried in the newly turned
soil. It was something like a ring of rusty iron or brass, and when the
robin flew up into a tree near by she put out her hand and picked the
ring up. It was more than a ring, however; it was an old key which
looked as if it had been buried a long time.

Mistress Mary stood up and looked at it with an almost frightened
face as it hung from her finger.

'Perhaps it has been buried for ten years,' she said in a whisper.
'Perhaps it is the key to the garden!'

She looked at the key quite a long time. She turned it over and
over, and thought about it… If it was the key to the closed garden,
and she could find out where the door was, she could perhaps open
it and see what was inside the walls, and what had happened to the
old rose trees. It was because it had been shut up so long that she
wanted to see it. It seemed as if it must be different from other

79

places and that something strange must have happened to it during ten years. Besides that, if she liked it she could go into it every day and shut the door behind her, and she could make up some play of her own and play it quite alone, because nobody would ever know where she was, but would think the door was still locked and the key buried in the earth. The thought of that pleased her very much.

Living, as it were, all by herself in a house with a hundred mysteriously closed rooms and having nothing whatever to do to amuse herself, had set her inactive brain to working and was actually awakening her imagination. There is no doubt that the fresh, strong, pure air from the moor had a great deal to do with it. Just as it had given her an appetite, and fighting with the wind had stirred her blood, so the same things had stirred her mind. In India she had always been too hot and languid and weak to care much about anything, but in this place she was beginning to care and to want to do new things. Already she felt less 'contrary', though she did not know why.

She put the key in her pocket and walked up and down her walk. No one but herself ever seemed to come there, so she could walk slowly and look at the wall, or, rather, at the ivy growing on it. The ivy was the baffling thing. Howsoever carefully she looked she could see nothing but thickly growing, glossy, dark green leaves. She was very much disappointed. Something of her contrariness came back to her as she paced the wall and looked over it at the tree-tops inside. It seemed so silly, she said to herself, to be near it and not be able to get in. She took the key in her pocket when she went back to the house, and she made up her mind that she would always carry it with her when she went out, so that if she ever should find the hidden door she would be ready.

Mrs Medlock had allowed the housemaid, Martha, to sleep all night at her cottage home, but she was back at her work in the morning with cheeks redder than ever and in the best of spirits...

She was full of stories of the delights of her day out. Her mother had been glad to see her and they had got the baking and washing all out of the way. She had even made each of the children a dough-cake with a bit of brown sugar in it...

In the evening they had all sat round the fire, and Martha and her mother had sewed patches on torn clothes and mended stockings and Martha had told them about the little girl who had come from

India and who had been waited on all her life by what Martha called 'blacks' until she didn't know how to put on her own stockings.

'Eh! they did like to hear about you,' said Martha. 'They wanted to know all about th' blacks an' about th' ship you came in. I couldn't tell 'em enough...'

Presently Martha went out of the room and came back with something held in her hands under her apron.

'What does tha' think,' she said, with a cheerful grin. 'I've brought thee a present.'

'A present!' exclaimed Mistress Mary. How could a cottage full of fourteen hungry people give anyone a present!

'A man was drivin' across the moor peddlin',' Martha explained. 'An' he stopped his cart at our door. He had pots an' pans an' odds an' ends, but Mother had no money to buy anythin'. Just as he was goin' away our 'Lizabeth Ellen called out, "Mother, he's got skippin'-ropes with red an' blue handles." An' Mother she calls out quite sudden, "Here, stop, mister! How much are they?" An' he says "Tuppence", an' Mother she began fumblin' in her pocket an' she says to me, "Martha, tha's brought thee thy wages like a good lass, an' I've got four places to put every penny, but I'm just goin' to take tuppence out of it to buy that child a skippin'-rope", an' she bought one an' here it is.'

She brought it out from under her apron and exhibited it quite proudly. It was a strong, slender rope with a striped red and blue handle at each end, but Mary Lennox had never seen a skipping-rope before. She gazed at it with a mystified expression.

'What is it for?' she asked curiously.

'For!' cried out Martha. 'Does tha' mean that they've not got skippin'-ropes in India, for all they've got elephants and tigers and camels!... This is what it's for; just watch me.'

And she ran into the middle of the room and, taking a handle in each hand, began to skip, and skip, and skip. The interest and curiosity in Mistress Mary's face delighted her, and she went on skipping and counted as she skipped until she had reached a hundred.

'I could skip longer than that,' she said when she stopped. 'I've skipped as much as five hundred when I was twelve, but I wasn't as fat then as I am now, an' I was in practice.'

Mary got up from her chair beginning to feel excited herself.

'It looks nice,' she said. 'Your mother is a kind woman. Do you
think I could ever skip like that?'

'You just try it,' urged Martha, handing her the skipping-rope.
'You can't skip a hundred at first, but if you practise you'll mount up.
That's what Mother said. She says, "Nothin' will do her more good
than skippin'-rope. It's th' sensiblest toy a child can have. Let her
play out in th' fresh air skippin' an' it'll stretch her legs an' arms an'
give her some strength in 'em." '

It was plain that there was not a great deal of strength in Mistress
Mary's arms and legs when she first began to skip. She was not very
clever at it, but she liked it so much that she did not want to stop.

'Put on tha' things and run an' skip out o' doors,' said Martha.
'Mother said I must tell you to keep out o' doors as much as you
could, even when it rains a bit, so as tha' wrap up warm.'

Mary put on her coat and hat and took her skipping-rope over her
arm. She opened the door to go out, and then suddenly thought of
something and turned back rather slowly.

'Martha,' she said, 'they were your wages. It was your twopence
really. Thank you.' She said it stiffly because she was not used to
thanking people or noticing that they did things for her. 'Thank you,'
she said, and held out her hand because she did not know what else
to do.

Martha gave her hand a clumsy little shake, as if she was not
accustomed to this sort of thing either. Then she laughed.

'Eh! tha' art a queer, old-womanish thing,' she said. 'If tha'd been
our 'Lizabeth Ellen tha'd have give me a kiss.'

Mary looked stiffer than ever.

'Do you want me to kiss you?'

Martha laughed again.

'Nay, not me,' she answered. 'If tha' was different, p'raps tha'd
want to thysel'. But tha' isn't. Run off outside an' play with thy rope.'

Mistress Mary felt a little awkward as she went out of the room.
Yorkshire people seemed strange, and Martha was always rather a
puzzle to her. At first she had disliked her very much, but now she
did not.

The skipping-rope was a wonderful thing. She counted and
skipped, and skipped and counted, until her cheeks were quite red,
and she was more interested than she had ever been since she was
born. The sun was shining and a little wind was blowing – not a

rough wind, but one which came in delightful little gusts and brought a fresh scent of newly turned earth with it. She skipped round the fountain garden, and up one walk and down another. She skipped at last into the kitchen garden and saw Ben Weatherstaff digging and talking to his robin, which was hopping about him. She skipped down the walk toward him and he lifted his head and looked at her with a curious expression. She had wondered if he would notice her. She really wanted him to see her skip.

'Well!' he exclaimed. 'Upon my word! P'raps tha' art a young 'un, after all, an' p'raps tha's got child's blood in thy veins instead of sour buttermilk. Tha's skipped red into thy cheeks as sure as my name's Ben Weatherstaff. I wouldn't have believed tha' could do it.'

'I never skipped before,' Mary said. 'I'm just beginning. I can only go up to twenty.'

'Tha' keep on,' said Ben. 'Tha' shapes well enough at it for a young 'un that's lived with heathen. Just see how he's watchin' thee,' jerking his head towards the robin. 'He followed after thee yesterday. He'll be at it again today. He'll be bound to find out what th' skippin'-rope is. He's never seen one. Eh!' shaking his head at the bird, 'tha' curiosity will be th' death of thee some time if tha' doesn't look sharp.'

Mary skipped round all the gardens and round the orchard, resting every few minutes. At length she went to her own special walk and made up her mind to try if she could skip the whole length of it. It was a good long skip and she began slowly, but before she had gone half-way down the path she was so hot and breathless that she was obliged to stop. She did not mind much, because she had already counted up to thirty. She stopped with a little laugh of pleasure, and there, lo and behold, was the robin swaying on a long branch of ivy. He had followed her and he greeted her with a chirp. As Mary had skipped toward him she felt something heavy in her pocket strike against her at each jump, and when she saw the robin she laughed again.

'You showed me where the key was yesterday,' she said. 'You ought to show me the door today; but I don't believe you know!'

The robin flew from his swinging spray of ivy on to the top of the wall and he opened his beak and sang a loud, lovely trill, merely to show off. Nothing in the world is quite as adorably lovely as a robin when he shows off – and they are nearly always doing it.

Mary Lennox had heard a great deal about Magic in her Ayah's stories, and she always said that what happened almost at that moment was Magic.

One of the nice little gusts of wind rushed down the walk, and it was a stronger one than the rest. It was strong enough to wave the branches of the trees, and it was more than strong enough to sway the trailing sprays of untrimmed ivy hanging from the wall. Mary had stepped close to the robin, and suddenly the gust of wind swung aside some loose ivy trails, and more suddenly still she jumped toward it and caught it in her hand. This she did because she had seen something under it – a round knob which had been covered by the leaves hanging over it. It was the knob of a door.

She put her hands under the leaves and began to pull and push them aside. Thick as the ivy hung, it nearly all was a loose and swinging curtain, though some had crept over wood and iron. Mary's heart began to thump and her hands to shake a little in her delight and excitement. The robin kept singing and twittering away and tilting his head on one side, as if he were as excited as she was. What was this under her hands which was square and made of iron and which her fingers found a hole in?

It was the lock of the door which had been closed ten years and she put her hand in her pocket, drew out the key and found it fitted the keyhole. She put the key in and turned it. It took two hands to do it, but it did turn.

And then she took a long breath and looked behind her up the long walk to see if anyone was coming. No one was coming. No one ever did come, it seemed, and she took another long breath, because she could not help it, and she held back the swinging curtain of ivy and pushed back the door which opened slowly – slowly.

Then she slipped through it, and shut it behind her, and stood with her back against it, looking about her and breathing quite fast with excitement, and wonder, and delight.

She was standing *inside* the secret garden.

'A Shetland Prayer'

JANINE RILEY (AGED 9)

Thankdee lorde fur da sun an raen dat maks da
tatties, neeps an a da veegetebles dat grow.
An keeps wis lifen. An da fish wir faders cetch an
da ots da crofters grow fur da oneemals
dat gees wis milk on mit a thankdee lorde
fur da plants dat maks wir yeards a bonny.

This is Shetland dialect. Here is the translation:

Thank you Lord for the sun and rain
that makes the potatoes, turnips and
all the vegetables that grow
and keeps us living.
And the fish our fathers catch
and the oats the crofters grow for
the animals
that give us milk and meat.
I thank you Lord for the plants
That make our gardens beautiful.

Switch on the Night

RAY BRADBURY

Once there was a little boy
who didn't like the Night.

He liked
lanterns and lamps
and
torches and tapers
and
beacons and bonfires
and
flashlights and flares.
But he didn't like the Night.

You saw him in
parlours and pantries
and
cellars and cupboards
and
attics and alcoves
and
hollering in halls.
But you never saw him outside...
in the Night.

He didn't like light-switches at all.
Because light-switches turned off
the yellow lamps
the green lamps
the white lamps
the hall lights

the house lights
the lights in all the rooms.
He wouldn't touch a light-switch.

And he wouldn't go out to play
after dark.
He was very lonely.
And unhappy.
For he saw, from his window,
the other children playing
on the summer-night lawns.
In and out of the dark and
lamplight ran the children...
happily.

But where was our little boy?
Up in his room.
With his lanterns and lamps
and flashlights
and candles and chandeliers.
All by himself.

He liked only the sun.
The yellow sun.
He didn't like
the Night.

When it was time for Mother and Father
to walk around switching off all the
lights...
One by one.
One by one.
The porch lights
the parlour lights
the pale lights
the pink lights
the pantry lights
and stair lights...
Then the little boy hid in his bed.

Late at night
his was the only room
with a light
in all the town.

And then one night
With his father away on a trip
And his mother gone to bed early,
The little boy wandered alone,
All alone through the house.

My, how he had the lights blazing!
the parlour lights
and porch lights
the pantry lights
the pale lights
the pink lights
the hall lights
the kitchen lights
even the *attic* lights!
The house looked like it was on fire!

But still the little boy was alone.
While the other children played
on the night lawns.
Laughing.
Far away.

All of a sudden he heard
a rap at a window!
Something dark was there.
A knock at the screen door.
Something dark was there!
A tap at the back porch.
Something dark was there!

And all of a sudden someone said, 'Hello!'
And a little girl stood there in the middle of

the white lights, the bright lights,
the hall lights, the small lights,
the yellow lights, the mellow lights.

'My name is Dark,' she said.
And she had dark hair,
and dark eyes,
and wore a dark dress
and dark shoes.
But her face was as white as the moon.
And the light in her eyes
shone like white stars.

'You're lonely,' she said.

'I want to run with the children outside,'
said the little boy. 'But I don't like the Night.'

'I'll introduce you to the Night,' said Dark.
'And you'll be friends.'
She put out a porch light.
'You see,' she said. 'It's not switching
off the light. No, not at all!
It's simply switching *on* the Night.
You can turn the Night off and on, just like
you can turn a light off and on.
With the same switch!' she said.

'I never thought of that,' the little boy said.

'And when you switch on the Night,' said Dark,
'why, you switch on the *crickets*!
And you switch on the frogs!
And you switch on the stars!
The light stars
the bright stars
the true stars
the blue stars!

Heaven is a house
with porch lights
and parlour lights
pink lights and pantry lights
red lights
green lights
blue lights
yellow lights
flashlights
candle lights
and hall lights!'

'Who can hear the crickets with the lights on?'
Nobody.
'Who can hear the frogs with the lights on?'
Nobody.
'Who can see the stars with the lights on?'
Nobody.
'Who can see the moon with the lights on?'
Nobody.

'Think what you're missing!
Have you ever thought of
switching on the crickets,
switching on the frogs,
switching on the stars,
and the great big white moon?'

'No,' said the little boy.

'Well, try it,' said Dark.
And they did.

They climbed up and down stairs,
switching on the Night.
Switching on the dark.
Letting the Night live in every room.
Like a frog.
Or a cricket.

Or a star.
Or a moon.

And they switched on the crickets.
And they switched on the frogs.
And they switched on the white, ice-cream moon.

'Oh, I like this!' said the little boy.
'Can I switch on the Night always?'

'Of course!' said Dark, the little girl.
And then she vanished.

And now the little boy is very happy.
He likes the Night.
Now he has a Night-switch instead of
a light-switch!
He likes switches now.
He threw away his candles
and flashlights
and lamplights.
And any night in summer that you wish
you can see him

Switching on the white moon,
switching on the red stars,
switching on the blue stars,
the green stars, the light stars,
the white stars,
switching on the frogs, the crickets, and Night.

And running in the dark, on the lawns,
with the happy children...
Laughing.

'High Tide'

MARGARET BELL (AGED 7)

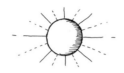

The tide rushes in, then it falls
The wind is whistling then it calls
To the mossy harbour walls
    And the docks
The waves are crashing on the shore.
The grey seals hear a deafening roar
While over them the seagulls soar
    From the rocks
Here you see the sleek seals play
On the sandbank in the bay,
Splashing each other in the spray
    Having fun.
Here you see a crab keep cool,
Bathing in a rocky pool.
Pebbles sparkle just like jewels
    In the sun.
In a cranny sparkling bright
Where you see the stars at night
A golden starfish reflects the light
    As he lolls.
Out at sea the herring glide.
While the mackerel try to hide
From fishing boats in the high tide
    With their trawls.
Little new born wavelets bring
Mussels, cockles and whelks that cling
To build a throne for the sea king
    In the sea.
Fishermen in boats go by
And hang their big nets out to dry.
While clouds make patterns in the sky
Just for me.

5
Who Cares?

Does the One who made the world care for it still? I believe so.
We know that many people care too, as these
next poems and stories all show.
The Lion's Tale asks the question, who's in charge? Resourceful
Zilya comes up with a plan to save her valley. The Very
Worried Sparrow hears some good news. The Lost Princess,
from the famous story *The Snow Goose*, is cared for by Frith and
a lonely disabled man called Rhayader. And the missing boy
in *Angel Train* discovers the truth of the last poem in this
section – 'He's got the whole world in his hands'.

'God Who Made the Earth'

SARAH BETTS RHODES

God who made the earth,
The air, the sky, the sea,
Who gave the light its birth,
Careth for me.

God who made the grass,
The flower, the fruit, the tree,
The day and night to pass,
Careth for me.

God who made the sun,
The moon, the stars, is he
Who, when life's clouds come on,
Careth for me.

The Lion's Tale

From *Tales from the Ark*

AVRIL ROWLANDS

God has put Mr Noah, a man who confesses he's
scared of spiders, in charge of his rescue-ship, the ark,
with its cargo of animals…

Mr Noah and his family, and two of every animal, insect and bird spent the first night safe inside the wooden ark, which God had told Mr Noah to make to save them from the flood.

But although they were safe, none of them slept well.

Mr Noah tossed and turned and had bad dreams about being drowned in the flood or eaten by an animal. Some of the animals were very noisy sleepers and kept waking him up. All night there was hissing, sighing, rumbling, muttering, squawking, squeaking, trumpeting and bellowing. It was all very disturbing.

The lion did not sleep well either. He paced angrily up and down his stall, his great tail thumping the floor behind him.

'I protest,' he said to his wife. 'I protest most strongly.'

'Mmm…?' said his wife, who was trying to sleep.

'*I* should have been put in charge of this whole operation. God should have given *me* the job. I can control the animals better than Mr Noah. Aren't I the most powerful of all the beasts? Aren't I King of the jungle?'

'Yes, dear,' said his wife sleepily. 'But we're not in the jungle now.'

The lion stopped. 'Of course we are,' he said. 'Everywhere's a jungle and only the strongest and toughest survive.' He started pacing once more, swishing his great tail from side to side. 'Only the strongest and toughest *deserve* to survive,' he added.

'Oh do be quiet and go to sleep,' his wife said. 'And stop pacing up and down. You're making me dizzy.'

The following morning Mr Noah was just getting out of bed when there was a tap on the door of his cabin.

'Yes?' he called out sharply, in rather a bad temper because of the sleepless night. 'Who is it?'

The lion stuck his head round the door.

'I thought I ought to advise you,' he said in a majestic sort of voice, 'as you are *supposed* to be in charge here – that some of the animals are attempting to eat each other. Whether or not you can stop them is another matter. *I* could, of course, but then I'm not in charge…'

He found himself speaking to an empty room, for Mr Noah had run straight out of the cabin. The lion sniffed in disgust.

'Well really,' he said. 'Some people have no manners, no manners at all.' He sniffed again. 'Anyway, I'm only the messenger, a creature of no importance.'

His eye fell on the key that was in the lock of Mr Noah's cabin door and a cunning smile spread across his face.

'No importance at all,' he said in quite a different voice and padded off after Mr Noah.

In the big hall Mr Noah was horrified by what he saw.

'Stop!' he shouted. 'Stop it at once, do you hear?'

'Why should we?' asked one of the leopards.

'We always hunt for our food,' added the other.

'But you don't need to,' said Mr Noah. 'The food's all provided.'

'What else are we meant to do to pass the time?' said one of the foxes.

'Well, I don't know, do I?' Mr Noah replied irritably, feeling tired, cross and rather silly when he realized he was dressed only in his nightshirt.

'Don't be such a spoilsport,' said the other fox, who was trying to coax a dormouse from its hiding place. 'It's all good fun and they *like* being hunted.'

'No, we don't,' said the dormouse, who was shivering with fright.

Mr Noah banged on the floor.

'This,' said Mr Noah loudly, 'has gone far enough! I shall make another rule: "Animals are strictly forbidden to eat one another while on this voyage." I'll get Shem to write it out and pin it up so that everyone can see.'

'But how many of us can read?' asked the monkey in a bored voice.

Mr Noah ignored this. 'I don't care what you do when we get back on dry land, but while we're in the ark you will all do as I say,' he said severely. 'Now behave yourselves while I go and get dressed.'

After he had gone the animals started muttering.

'Just who does he think he is?' asked the fox.

'God, most likely,' said the lion. He made his way through the teeming animals to the centre of the big hall. A window was set high up in the roof of the ark, and through it a shaft of sunlight shone on the deep gold of the lion's mane. He looked quite magnificent.

He called in a deep voice, 'Animals – fellow travellers – friends…!'

'You're no friend of mine,' said the dormouse quietly.

'As I see it,' the lion went on, 'we are stuck in this ark for an unknown length of time. One of us has to be in charge and that one should be the strongest amongst us. That is the law of the jungle, as I'm sure you'll all agree.'

Some of the animals thumped their tails on the floor.

'Now this Mr Noah,' the lion continued, 'he's a good enough human, as humans go, but he isn't the strongest. So why should he be in charge?'

'Perhaps he's clever,' said one of the giraffes, frowning in concentration. 'You've got to be clever to be in charge.'

'Very true,' agreed the lion. 'And perhaps Mr Noah is clever. But it's hardly clever of him to order us about, laying down the law, making up rules as and when he chooses – now is it?'

More animals thumped their tails and there were murmurs of agreement. The lion beamed his approval.

'But,' said the dormouse timidly. 'God put Mr Noah in charge.'

The lion looked annoyed.

'*If* God did that,' he said in his grandest manner, 'then God made a mistake.'

The tiger pricked up his ears. 'What are you up to?' he asked suspiciously.

'You'll see,' said the lion and turned and walked away.

While all this was going on in the big hall, Mr Noah was hurriedly getting dressed. As he did so, he talked to God.

'I'm not making a very good job of it, am I?' he asked humbly.

God smiled but said nothing.

'I thought,' Mr Noah went on, tying his belt round his waist, 'that if I showed them I was firm and not frightened – if I shouted a bit and laid down the law – then they'd behave properly. But I'm not sure they'll take any notice of me.'

Mr Noah put on his shoes. 'You put me in charge, God, so can't *you* do something about it? Can't you *make* them do what I say? It's for their own good.'

God sighed. 'I'm sorry, Noah. I don't rule by force.'

Noah was thinking about this when he heard a noise at the door of his cabin. He turned the handle, but the door would not open. He rattled it loudly, but the door remained firmly shut. It had been locked from the outside.

Mr Noah sat on his bed. 'What do I do, God?' he asked.

'Just wait,' said God. 'And think.'

The lion, well pleased with himself, walked back to the big hall. *That* took care of Mr Noah!

He stood in front of the crowd of animals. 'It's all sorted out,' he said. 'I'm in charge now.'

The tiger looked up. 'Who says?'

'I do,' said the lion, 'by virtue of being King of the jungle, Lord of all Beasts, strongest…' he stopped and smiled modestly, 'and cleverest…'

'And biggest-headed,' added the monkey sourly.

'Where's Mr Noah?' asked the tiger.

'Quite safe,' said the lion. 'No need to worry – I've dealt with him.'

98

He smiled again and the dormouse shuddered. 'You haven't *eaten* him… have you?' he asked faintly.

'Of course not,' said the lion.

'Yet,' he added.

The animals were silent.

'Now,' the lion went on briskly. 'As ruler here…'

The tiger snarled. 'Ruler?' he said. 'You? We'll soon see about that.'

He sprang at the lion and everyone scattered as the fight began. It was a fierce fight which raged up and down and round and round the big hall, bumping off walls and flattening the smaller animals who could not get out of the way in time. The ark groaned and shook.

Mr Noah, locked in his cabin, put his head in his hands, while Mrs Noah, Shem, Ham, Japheth and their wives, who were not locked in, were all far too frightened to come out.

The other animals were frightened too, and one by one they slipped out of the big hall and made their way to Mr Noah's cabin. Eventually they were all squashed in the corridor outside.

'I don't think I want to be ruled by the lion,' said the dormouse.

'Or the tiger,' bleated one of the goats.

'Can't we ask Mr Noah to take charge again?' suggested the dormouse.

The goat put his face to the keyhole.

'Mr Noah, we've been thinking. We'd like you to be in charge, so will you please come and stop the lion and tiger fighting.'

Mr Noah jumped off the bed and went to the door. 'Well, yes,' he said. 'Of course. But I'm locked in.'

A minute later he heard the key being turned in the lock, the door opened and he was free.

Mr Noah led the procession back to the big hall. As they drew nearer the animals grew silent, listening anxiously for the sounds of fighting, but everything was quiet. Too quiet.

'Perhaps they've killed each other,' said the goat hopefully.

'Oh, I do hope not,' said Mr Noah and quickened his pace. He marched into the hall, then stopped abruptly, staring in amazement. The animals crowded round.

In front of them, side by side, lay the lion and the tiger. Worn out with fighting, they were both fast asleep and snoring gently.

The goat started to snigger, then the dormouse began squeaking and soon all the animals, insects and birds were laughing. Their laughter woke the lion and tiger.

'What – what happened?' asked the lion, hurriedly getting to his feet and snarling at the tiger.

'I think,' said the tiger with dignity, 'that the fight was a draw.'

Just then the lion caught sight of Mr Noah. 'What are you doing here?' he asked. 'You should be locked in your cabin.'

The monkey pushed his way to the front, the key dangling from his long fingers. 'You might be strong,' he said, 'but you're not so clever. You left the key on the floor.'

The animals began laughing again.

'The animals came and asked me to take charge,' Mr Noah said mildly.

'Oh,' said the lion uncomfortably, 'I see.'

Mr Noah felt sorry for him. 'Look, I have an apology to make. I thought I could rule you all by shouting and laying down the law. But God doesn't rule like that and I shouldn't have tried.'

He looked at the lion. 'I'm not as strong as you, or the tiger, and I'm not very clever, but I'm very glad you locked me in because it made me talk to God and do some thinking. If we're going to survive this trip we've got to work together. So can we start again?' He put out his hand. 'Will you be my assistant, lion – and tiger, will you be my other assistant?'

There was a moment's pause before the lion said graciously, 'All right. I agree.'

'Me too,' said the tiger hurriedly.

The lion raised its great head and looked round at the animals, who were all pressing eagerly against Mr Noah in order not to miss anything.

'Come along now,' said the lion in a grand voice. 'Give Mr Noah some room. Show some respect for the man God put in charge.'

The animals moved back and the lion left the hall in a stately fashion. Mr Noah sighed and followed. The tiger gave a crooked smile and went to his stall, while the animals, insects and birds all went to their various perching, nesting and sleeping places, and peace fell on the ark.

'On Another's Sorrow'

An Extract

WILLIAM BLAKE

And can he who smiles on all
Hear the wren with sorrows small,
Hear the small bird's grief and care,
Hear the woes that infants bear,

And not sit beside the nest,
Pouring pity in their breast;
And not sit the cradle near,
Weeping tear on infant's tear;

And not sit both night and day,
Wiping all our tears away?
O, no! never can it be!
Never, never can it be!

The Very Worried Sparrow

MERYL DONEY

There was once a Very Worried Sparrow. All the other birds looked up at the bright blue sky and sang for joy. But the Very Worried Sparrow hung his head and shut his beak tight. He did look unhappy. He had always worried, even when he was just a baby bird in the nest. His brothers and sisters kept saying, 'Cheep, cheep, cheer up!' But the Very Worried Sparrow only said, 'Meep, meep, oh dear!'

When he began to grow, the first thing he thought about was food.

'Oh dear, oh dear!' he thought. 'I'm so hungry, whatever am I going to eat?'

His brothers and sisters did not seem to worry at all. They just sat in the nest, looking up at the tree and the bright blue sky.

'It's because they don't think,' he said to himself.

Suddenly there was a whirr of wings and his mother was back with four fat juicy caterpillars in her beak.

'Cheep, cheep, cheep,' went all the baby birds, and she popped a caterpillar into each mouth.

Very soon the babies were quite fat and their feathers had begun to grow. So Father bird said, 'I think it's time you all learned to fly.'

'Cheep, cheep, hooray!' they all chorused – all, that is, except the Very Worried Sparrow.

He said, 'Meep, meep, oh dear!' and looked more worried than ever.

The sparrows hopped out of the nest on to a big branch. They sat in a line bravely flapping their wings. Father and Mother birds flew to a nearby fence and called to them. One by one the sparrows set off.

'Wheeeeeee, this is lovely,' they called.

The Very Worried Sparrow hopped from one foot to the other. 'I'll never do it,' he cheeped to himself. 'Oh dear!'

He was so frightened, he lost his balance and toppled off the branch. He gulped, opened his little wings wide – and flew!

'There,' said his mother as he landed beside her. 'You can do it, too.'

As the spring days turned into warm summer the little birds grew and grew. They learned to find caterpillars among the green leaves. Snip-snap went their busy beaks. They searched for seeds and berries on the brown earth. Best of all they learned to sing. The world was filled with happy chirping.

All except the Very Worried Sparrow. He was not as brave as the others.

'It's such a big place out there,' he thought. 'I might get lost. Meep, meep, oh dear!' And he looked more unhappy than ever.

At dusk, when they were settling down for the night, Father sparrow gathered them all together, warm and snug in the nest. He began to tell them wonderful stories of long ago and far away:

> *of the Great Father who made the world*
> *and everything in it;*
> *of how the day begins,*
> *and where the wind comes from,*
> *and all the little things*
> *that every creature knows.*

The young birds listened with bright eyes.

All except the Very Worried Sparrow. He was too worried to listen, and too afraid. He peered out into the darkness until, very slowly, his eyes closed and he fell asleep.

By mid-summer the Very Worried Sparrow felt a bit braver. He set off from home, flying here and there, looking for food – and worrying about where to find it. The open fields looked a good place. The early corn had just been cut and golden grains lay among the stubble.

Suddenly a shadow rushed across the ground. The little sparrow felt his heart go 'bump'. Above him hovered the terrible Sparrowhawk.

His heart beat so fast he was too frightened even to worry! He crouched down small and still, and waited.

There was a rush of wings as the Sparrowhawk struck. When the sparrow opened his eyes he saw the hawk flying up and away from him. He held a small field-mouse in his great claw.

'Ooooooooh dear!' breathed the Very Worried Sparrow, feeling quite weak. 'Oh dear, oh dear!' As soon as he felt better he flew home as fast as his wings would carry him.

After that, the little sparrow looked more worried than ever. The autumn winds blew and the trees shed their leaves.

'Oh dear,' thought the Very Worried Sparrow. 'It's getting colder and colder. How shall I keep warm?'

At night the frost came. And then the snow fell, covering the ground in a soft layer of sparkling white. The water in the bird tables in the gardens turned to ice. Puddles and ponds froze solid.

'Oh dear,' thought the Very Worried Sparrow. 'How am I going to find food to eat and water to drink?'

But he did. There was one little pond so sheltered that it didn't freeze. Every day the sparrow joined the other birds drinking at the pond.

He had to look hard, but he could still find seeds on the bare earth and berries on the hedges. Later on, the children in the nearby house began to scatter bread each morning on the snow-covered grass in the garden. The waiting sparrows swooped down in a rush and chirped and quarrelled over it.

Spring came at last and the snow melted away into the grass. The sun shone through the water dripping from twigs and roofs and made them sparkle. The sparrows were very excited.

'It will soon be nesting time,' they said, and began to look around for partners.

The girl sparrows giggled and whispered on the branches while the boy sparrows flew and swooped and sang, just to show off. Soon there were pairs of birds, everywhere, searching for a good place to build their nests.

'Oh dear!' thought the Very Worried Sparrow. 'Now what shall I do? No one will want me for a mate.' Sadly he flew off by himself.

He settled in a small apple tree at the far end of the garden. But he found there was someone there already. It was another sparrow and she looked very shy.

'Cheep,' she said, in a small voice.

'Meep, meep,' said the Very Worried Sparrow. But he felt more hopeful.

'Will you be my mate?' he asked, all in a rush.

'Oh, yes,' said the shy little sparrow, and she smiled at him.

At first, the sparrow and his mate were very happy. They flew around the garden together, as the spring sun grew warmer and warmer. But after a while the Very Worried Sparrow started to worry again.

'Where shall we build our nest?' he thought. 'The others have taken the best places. I'll never find somewhere quiet and safe.'

The shy little sparrow flew back to the small apple tree at the far end of the garden. 'Look,' she chirped, 'no one has started to build here yet, and it's very quiet and safe.'

'So it is,' said the Very Worried Sparrow. And he looked a bit happier. 'We must begin to build at once.'

The apple blossom fell and new green leaves hid the nest from sight. Before long the shy little sparrow was sitting on the nest, looking very proud. Under her warm feathers were four beautiful

eggs. Her mate was flying backwards and forwards, feeding her with tasty titbits. He should have been happy, but instead he was looking very, very… worried.

'Meep, meep, oh dear!' he chirped. 'I hope my eggs are safe. A cat might come. Or a hawk! The tree might fall. And how shall I feed the babies?'

'Roo, cooooo. What's the matter?' asked a gentle voice. It was a turtle-dove, with soft feathers and a very kindly look in her eyes. 'I've never seen a sparrow look so worried before.'

'Well,' said the sparrow, sighing, 'there are such a lot of things to worry about.' And a big tear rolled down his beak and splashed onto his claw.

'Roo, coo,' called the dove gently. 'Don't you know about the Great Father who made us all? Haven't you been listening to the stories of long ago and far away?'

'Well no,' sniffed the sparrow. 'I was too worried to listen.'

'The Great Father made us,' cooed the dove. 'He made us and he knows all about us. He looks after us and gives us all we need. He even knows when our time has come to leave the earth. Roo, coo.'

'Oh,' chirped the sparrow, and his eyes were round with surprise. 'I didn't know that.'

'When you were a baby bird, didn't you always have food?' asked the dove.

'Why yes,' said the sparrow.

'And when you learnt to fly, you didn't get hurt.'

'No, I didn't,' said the sparrow, thinking back.

'What about the Sparrowhawk?' the dove cooed gently. 'Your time had not yet come, had it?'

'I suppose not,' said the sparrow.

'And your food and water, your mate and your nest – and those beautiful eggs, they all came in good time, didn't they?'

'Yes, yes, they did!' chirped the sparrow, beginning to look much happier.

'Will you come home with me please?' he said to the dove. 'Come and tell us more. I promise I will listen this time.'

And so the dove flew to the apple tree at the bottom of the garden and perched on the branch next to the nest. As the sun set slowly over the hill, and all the birds were settling for sleep, the dove told the sparrows the stories of long ago and far away:

of the Great Father who made the world
and everything in it;
of how the day begins,
and where the wind comes from
and all the little things
that every creature knows.

She spoke of the seasons and the years, of how things grow and new life comes. She told how the Great Father knows each creature and its time on the earth.

Next day, when the sun rose, everything looked sparkling new in the morning light. The flowers opened their faces to the sun and all the birds were singing.

There was a little noise from the nest.

'Tock, tock, tock,' went one of the eggs. 'Tock, tock, tock, tock!'

'It's one of our babies,' cried the shy little sparrow excitedly. 'Today is the day they will hatch.'

Then the Very Worried Sparrow… smiled.

'I can't wait to see them,' he said. 'We can feed them and watch them grow and teach them to fly. There are so many things to do. And I want to tell them about the Great Father who made the world and everything in it, and who knows each sparrow. Then they won't have to worry for a single day.'

And he flapped his wings and sang for joy with all the other birds.

'Cheep, cheep, cheep,' he sang. 'Cheep, cheep, cheep' – loud enough to burst with happiness.

'The Little Things'

ANNE BELL

On nights when storms run wild,
And thunder tramples the stars,
When lightning startles the wakeful eye
Pity the little things;
The soft-breasted pigeon, rocked
On a brittle nest of too-few sticks;
Wren and thornbill and finch;
All creatures crouched in bending crops;
Hare and mouse and freckled quail;
All things that have no roof save storm –
On nights like these,
Pray for the little things.

Debbie, Sandy and Pepe

From *The Best Present and Other Stories*

MERRILL CORNEY

Debbie ran down the path beside the house.

'Look, Sandy! Come and have a look at this!' She knelt beside the little bundle of feathers on the ground and gently touched it with her finger. Sandra appeared beside her.

'It's a baby bird,' she said. 'It must have fallen out of its nest,' and she craned her neck upwards to search the tree above their heads.

'Poor little thing,' crooned Debbie as she stroked the shivering bundle. 'Your mother must be so worried.' She scooped it up in one hand and straight away it spread its tiny half-feathered wings and tried to fly. Its beak opened wide and it let out a squeaking, much louder than you would expect from such a small body.

'Look at its beak,' Sandra said, laughing. 'It's so big!'

'It looks like yellow plastic,' giggled Debbie. She wriggled her finger like a worm and the little creature snapped harmlessly at her.

Debbie stood up.

'We'd better find its nest and put it back,' she said. They searched every tree and bush in the garden, but there was no sign of a nest. No mother bird's cry of alarm broke the afternoon stillness.

'Perhaps he fluttered here from somewhere else,' suggested Sandra, 'and his mother couldn't find him.'

Debbie cradled him against her chest.

'Well, we'll just have to look after him ourselves then,' she said. 'We'll make a soft nest for him and feed him and when he grows up he will stay in our garden.'

They spent the rest of the afternoon caring for the bird. They chose the old letterbox in the hedge for a nest. It was part of the front fence, but the cypress hedge had grown over it so that the postman could not reach it. Now he put the mail in the new box shaped like a house that sat on the gatepost.

The girls half-filled the old box with dry grass clippings. It made a soft comfortable nest. The half-fledged, ugly little creature nestled down with eyes closed, then jerked its beak open and squawked for food.

'What do you think he eats, Sandy? Worms?'

'I reckon.'

They dug up worms with the garden trowel and deposited them in a squirming heap on the path. Sandra looked doubtfully at the writhing mass of worms busily trying to tie themselves in knots.

'They should really be mushed up, shouldn't they?' she asked.

'I bags not doing it! You do it, Sandy,' Debbie said, shuddering.

'Perhaps we could use Mum's blender!' Sandra's eyebrows shot up with the effort of producing such a good idea.

'Yuk! That's revolting! And think of the poor worms!' Debbie put her hands on her hips. 'He'll just have to learn to eat them whole!'

Sandra held a twisting worm close to his beak. He snapped it up, closed his eyes and swallowed, but the worm fell out unharmed.

'Maybe they eat other things as well,' said Debbie in a worried voice.

They thought for a minute.

'I bet he's the type that eats flies and mozzies!' announced Sandra.

'And grass seeds and things,' added Debbie.

By the time Mum called them in to tea, they had collected quite a supply of insects and seeds. The bird did his best to eat something, but it was hard to tell if anything went down or not. Sandy felt in her pocket and brought out a dusty piece of chocolate. She broke off a teeny piece with her fingernail.

'Try this,' she said and pushed it into his open beak. He didn't seem to like it much, so she ate the rest. They filled a bottle top with water and placed it carefully in a corner so that it would not spill, and bedded him down for the night. He seemed quite content in his letterbox nest.

'Good night, Pepe,' whispered Debbie.

'How do you know his name's Pepe?' asked Sandra.

'I don't. He just makes a noise like that,' said Debbie and closed down the lid of the box.

They told Mum all about him at tea-time and took her out to see him.

'When he grows up can we keep him?' Debbie pleaded.

'Yes, Mum, we could get a cage for him,' Sandra added.

'Birds are happier outside, being free,' said their mum. 'He wouldn't be happy inside a cage.'

Debbie lay awake a long time that night. She could remember how warm and soft he was; how fragile and delicate his bones felt under the feathers. Rather ugly. And that oversized yellow plastic beak taking up all his face – but she knew that when he grew up he would be very handsome. He would live in the garden and every morning and evening he would come pecking on her window. She would let him in and he would fly around the room, then settle on her shoulder and feed from her hand.

'I could tie notes to his legs and send messages to my friends like they used to do with pigeons during the war,' she thought. It made her feel warm and sleepy and excited and contented all at the same time.

Pepe didn't seem to have eaten any of his food when they visited him next morning. He just put his head on one side and winked at them with his bright little eyes when they peered into the box.

Debbie couldn't concentrate on her lessons that day. Her mind was filled with plans for Pepe. She and Sandra met behind the shelter shed at lunchtime and spent most of the break searching for fresh worms, insects and seeds.

When the final bell rang that afternoon, Debbie was the first to the door. Mrs Atkins' hand fell heavily on her shoulder.

'What's the hurry, Debbie?'

'Oh, please, please, Mrs Atkins. I have to get home fast to feed this baby bird we found yesterday.' She had to explain it all to Mrs Atkins and, by the time she raced out the door, the playground was nearly deserted.

'Where have you been, Deb?' Sandra was swinging upside down on the monkey bars. 'I've been waiting for ages,' and she swung herself over and neatly landed on her feet. 'Have you got the worms?'

Debbie showed her the box banging up and down in her school bag and they hurried out the gate. When they got home she unslung the bag from her shoulder and pulled out the box of feed.

'Here comes your tea, Pepe,' she said as she pushed her way into the hedge.

'Is he cheeping?' Sandra wriggled in beside her. There was no sound as she lifted the lid of the letterbox.

'He must be asleep,' said Debbie. 'Here, hold the box a minute,' and she passed the precious food store to Sandra. The little bird lay on his side on the straw. His eyes and beak were shut.

'Come on, little Pepe,' whispered Debbie. 'Time to wake up.'

She reached in and gently slid her hand under the tiny body and lifted him out. He was cold and stiff.

'Oh, no,' she wailed. 'He's dead.'

'Let's have a look.' Sandra touched the bird's head. 'Yep, he's dead all right. Probably starved, I reckon. He hasn't eaten his food at all.' She paused. 'Where are we going to bury him?'

Debbie turned on her.

'Don't you even care?' she shouted. 'He was just a little baby. He was going to be our own special pet and now he's dead. I bet it was that chocolate you tried to feed him that killed him!' and she burst into tears.

'It's not my fault!' shouted Sandra. 'It probably would have died anyway. You're just stupid. You cry about everything! You even cried when Mum threw boiling water on the ants!' And Sandra stamped angrily inside.

Debbie knew it was true. She couldn't bear to think of anything suffering or dying. Mum said she was too soft-hearted for her own good. She wrapped the little bird in a tissue she found in her pocket, laid him under the hedge and covered him with fallen leaves.

'Goodbye, Pepe,' she whispered, then turned and, still sobbing, went into the house dragging her feet.

'Whatever is the matter, Deb?' Mum said, looking up from the stove where she was preparing dinner. 'Sandra told me about the bird. They are awfully hard to rear, Deb.' She put her arms around her daughter. 'Lots of them die. It's silly to get so upset about it. A big girl like you!'

Mum didn't understand, thought Debbie. It wasn't so much that things died, but that no-one seemed to care. Not like she did. It felt like a great weight on her heart. The little bird hadn't even had time to learn to fly. A small hope entered her mind. 'Do birds go to heaven, Mum?'

Her mother held her at arms length and looked at her.

'Goodness, what a question! How do I know? I don't even know if there is a God or not! Now – dry your eyes and stop thinking about it.'

She smiled at her and gave her a kiss on the forehead. 'Go and turn the calendar over for me. It's the first day of spring tomorrow.'

Debbie dried her eyes and, still sniffing, went to the calendar hanging on the wall above the sink. The new month had the usual pretty countryside scene. Debbie glanced at it and was about to turn away when she noticed for the first time a few lines of writing under the photograph. She bent closer and read:

Are not five sparrows sold for two pennies?
Yet not one of them is forgotten by God.

Not *one* of them? Debbie stared out the window. God knew *every* sparrow? The blue sky above the fence suddenly filled with a wheeling crowd of pigeons. A blackbird in the wattle tree tilted back his head and poured his song into the air against the background music of sparrows squabbling under the eaves. So many birds! Millions of them – and yet God knew and cared about each one.

'I'm not the only one who cares then, God, am I?' thought Debbie. 'There's me and you.' And suddenly it didn't seem to matter any more whether Pepe had gone to heaven or not. If God really cared, then everything would be all right.

She looked again at the calendar. The Bible quotation went on:

Indeed, the very hairs of your head are numbered.
Don't be afraid. You are worth more than
many sparrows.

With her ears full of bird song and the beating of many wings, Debbie ran and hugged her surprised mother.

'Don't worry, Mum,' she grinned, then, calling Sandra, she bounced down the back steps to play.

The Pigeon

JEAN SELBY

'Who's that?' Debbie leaned over to nudge her friend, Clare. They both stared across the desks at the new face. It was a pale, rather thin face, half hidden by a fall of dark hair.

The new girl sat alone, silent and still as a stone while the noisy tide of classroom life swirled round her.

'I wonder why she's come in the middle of term?' The fat and friendly Debbie was always curious about other people.

'Who cares?' Clare thumbed the pages of a magazine.

'Maybe we ought to make her welcome.'

'OK then. Later.' Clare reached for a last toffee as the teacher arrived.

At mid-morning break, boys and girls spilled out into the playground of the big comprehensive. Debbie and Clare kept well clear of the corner that was boys' territory. They had things to talk about that had to be kept secret.

The most important secret of the moment was Confirmation. They were both preparing to be confirmed at Easter. This, like singing in the church choir, was not something to be spread around in the school playground.

'My mum says I can have a gold cross and chain,' Debbie whispered excitedly.

'I've seen some super silver ones in the jeweller's,' said Clare. 'I think silver looks nicer. Anyway, we could go down town in the dinner break and look at them.'

'Good idea…' Debbie broke off. 'What's going on over there?' There was a noisy cluster of girls by the wall.

The two girls cruised over and found that the centre of attention was the new girl. She was being put through the usual cross-examination.

It seemed that her name was Mary, that she came from London, and that she and her mother were now living at Tickford, a village about four miles away. Apart from that she seemed unwilling to talk about herself.

'Are you a one-parent family?' someone asked.

'No!' Mary's pale face flushed.

'Where's your dad then? What's his job? Is he out of work?...'

Mary was rescued by the bell.

But Debbie was still curious.

'If you live at Tickford you must come in on our bus,' she whispered as they lined up. 'We're in the next village.'

'I bike in.'

'All that way!' Debbie stared.

Mary shrugged her shoulders.

'Come on!' Clare gave her inquisitive friend a shove. 'We're going in.'

The novelty of the new girl soon wore off. Mary merged into the classroom scene but remained a quiet, rather lonely figure. 'Boring' was the girls' verdict, and they left her alone.

Debbie and Clare made a half-hearted effort to be friendly but they didn't get very far.

'I don't think she wants friends,' Clare decided.

'Everybody wants friends.' The warm-hearted Debbie couldn't accept this. 'Let's try inviting her home to tea on Sunday or something.'

But it didn't work.

'I'm sorry, I can't,' Mary told them.

'What about the Sunday after?'

'No!' she shook her head. 'Not any Sunday.'

'What about Saturday then?' Debbie persisted.

'I have to help my mum.' Mary gave one of her rare smiles. 'Thanks, anyway.'

Debbie shrugged her shoulders and gave up. Loving your neighbour wasn't so easy when your neighbour didn't help!

The winter days lengthened into spring, and they all started counting the time till Easter holidays.

For Debbie and Clare Confirmation was near now, and the big secret to whisper about in the playground was what they were going to wear. They'd both been promised new dresses.

'I wish people still wore white,' said Debbie dreamily. 'My mum told me that girls used to wear long white dresses and veils.'

'Just like brides,' sighed Clare.

Suddenly a bunch of girls came by.

The boys are up to something over there,' they announced. 'We're going to see. Come on!' Debbie and Clare were swept along.

In the far corner of the playground a small grey pigeon was huddled against the wall. Darren Cox and his mob were throwing stones at it. From one wing, half spread out, came a trickle of blood.

'It can't fly!'

'They'll kill it!'

The girls stared, sickened by the sight.

'Why can't someone do something,' wailed Debbie.

Suddenly she found herself being pushed aside.

'Stop it! Stop it!' A voice powered by anger cut through the shouting and laughter.

'Would you believe, it's Mary!'

Mary the mouse, Mary the bore, Mary the quiet one, was tearing into the gang of boys.

She snatched up the wounded pigeon.

'You murdering pigs!' she blazed at them.

The attackers stood, suddenly still, hands loaded with stones. The onlookers, boys and girls, edged away and drew closer together. Mary was left facing Darren. There was a long silence. Then someone sniggered.

Darren's knuckles were white where he gripped his stone as he glared at the girl. Then, as Mary leaned over the pigeon, he saw the gleam of a silver chain round her neck.

'Look at that!' he yelled. 'She wears a cross. She's a flippin' Christian!'

'A do-gooder!' His mates took up the cry.

'A stupid animal lover!'

They moved closer as Mary stood up.

'Cowards!' she defied them. 'Bullies!' Holding the pigeon close against her she moved forward. Darren reached out to grab the chain. As he did so, a boy burst out of the crowd.

'Don't you touch her,' he yelled.

The next minute a scrum of boys and girls were pitching in. No one heard the bell go, and it finally took three masters to sort them all out. The hero of the day was the boy, David. The heroine, Mary, had disappeared.

'She went off on her bike,' someone told Debbie and Clare. 'She's got the pigeon in a box.'

On the bus home that evening the two girls were unusually quiet.

'You'd never guess she had guts like that,' said Clare.

'I suppose we ought to have had the courage to do what she did.' Debbie wriggled uncomfortably.

'Fight the good fight and all that.' Clare glanced over her shoulder to the back row of the bus where David and his friends were reading comics as though nothing had happened.

David was a stocky fair-haired boy whose parents kept the pub on the main road at the end of their village. Clare wondered what they were going to say when they saw him. His clothes were a disaster; there was a large bruise on his cheek, and his knuckles were grazed and cut. His friends were looking equally battered.

'I wonder what they'll tell their parents,' Clare remarked, but Debbie wasn't listening.

'I've had an idea,' she announced. 'As tomorrow's Saturday, let's bike out to Tickford in the afternoon and find Mary. I'd like to know she's okay and to tell her we think she's great.'

'Can't we tell her on Monday?' Clare didn't think it was a very good idea.

She thought even less of it when they actually got to Tickford and realized they hadn't a clue where to begin looking.

'It's such a small place someone's sure to know,' said Debbie cheerfully, eyeing the handful of houses in the main street. They tried young mums with prams. They tried old age pensioners who looked as though they'd been in the place for years, but none of them seemed to have heard of a teenager and her mum, newly arrived. They were about to give up when a farm labourer came to their rescue.

'You must mean those two at Nethercote Farm,' he told them. 'They're in a caravan up there.'

He set them on their way along a rough track.

'It's only about a mile,' he said cheerfully. 'You can't miss it.'

'Some mile!' Debbie puffed and groaned as they pedalled uphill over bumps and ruts. 'I can see why she comes to school on a bike. Think of walking all this way to the bus.'

'I wouldn't like to do it after dark, either.' Clare looked round at the empty spread of fields and woods.

'There it is!' Debbie pointed. They had reached the top of the rise and just below them to the left, the long flat roof of a caravan showed above the hedge. A wisp of smoke curled from its chimney.

As they came nearer they could see it was a shabby old trailer surrounded by an overgrown garden with a ramshackle collection of sheds, rabbit hutches and hen runs.

'There's Mary!' Debbie caught sight of the familiar figure. 'Hi!' she yelled.

Mary put down the two buckets she was carrying and swung round. As she did so, a big black and white collie leaped over the gate and bounded straight at them barking furiously.

They backed away from the snapping teeth.

'Rex!' A shrill whistle stopped the dog in its tracks. He crouched to the ground, his amber eyes fixed warily on the girls.

'Here!' Another whistle and the dog jumped up, swung round and disappeared again over the gate.

'Wish our dog was trained like that!' Clare thought of her own disorganized labrador.

'It's all right!' Mary called out. 'You can come in now.'

She stood quietly watching them, a slim figure in jeans and an old blue jersey. She seemed different somehow.

'I'm sorry about Rex.' She fondled the dog's ears as he sat close against her legs. 'He's my guard.'

'I should think you need it up here.' Clare glanced round at the desolate surroundings.

'We just came to see if you were OK – and the pigeon – and all that...' Debbie felt suddenly shy.

'The pigeon'll be OK. We set the wing.' Mary glanced toward the caravan. Was there a flicker of anxiety in her eyes, Debbie wondered? Her mother must be in there. Perhaps there was something wrong with her and she had to be kept hidden.

'Does it matter us coming to see you?' Clare broke the awkward silence.

Mary shook her head, but there was no mistaking now the anxious look in her eyes.

'I'd better go and tell mum.'

She moved away, the dog padding close at her heels.

'Do you think she's a witch?' Debbie whispered anxiously.

Mary's mum stepped out of the caravan. She was young and pretty with dark hair like Mary's and the same pale creamy skin, but there were dark shadows of tiredness under her eyes.

'You'll be staying to tea,' she said. 'Mary can show you the animals while I get it ready. We've another visitor coming, too,' she added with a smile.

At home, Mary seemed quite different from the quiet withdrawn girl they knew at school. Shyness melted away as they went round to meet the rabbits, the chickens and the new family of kittens in the hay shed.

'And this is my bird hospital.' Mary showed them a wire netting enclosure, where a pair of orphaned baby blackbirds were cosily housed in a little box. They watched Mary give them their food, dropping it carefully into the open yellow beaks. She handled them with a skill and confidence that deeply impressed Debbie.

'You've got a real way with animals,' she exclaimed.

'I love them,' said Mary simply. 'I'll bring the pigeon out here when she's stronger. We're keeping her indoors for the first day or two. Come and see.'

119

The inside of the shabby old caravan was a real surprise. It was bright, warm and welcoming.

'Mary's always been crazy about all creatures.' Her mother laughed as they crowded round the pigeon box. 'She can't bear to see an animal hurt.'

'We thought you were great yesterday.' Debbie wondered how much she had told her mother.

'Weren't you frightened?' asked Clare.

'I knew he'd take care of us.' Mary pointed to a picture of St Francis pinned above her bed. 'He's my favourite saint because he loved animals too… Yes,' she went on seeing the girls staring at the crucifix and the little painted figure of the Virgin on the ledge below the picture, 'we're Catholics.'

Debbie and Clare found themselves telling her about their confirmation. It felt good to share the secret.

'We're always scared the boys will find out,' confessed Clare.

Mary fingered the little silver cross round her neck.

'I'm not afraid of them knowing,' she said quietly. 'They can give you a bad time, but they can't take away the things you believe in.'

Debbie and Clare looked at each other and thought of the gold and silver crosses. Suddenly it didn't seem so important what they looked like. If they wore them they'd have to live up to them.

They were interrupted by a sudden explosion of barking from Rex.

'That'll be him!' Mary jumped up. Debbie and Clare glanced at each other.

To their astonishment, the boy who walked in was David. Mary's mum greeted him like an old friend.

'This is a real party,' she said gaily as she put a fat brown teapot on the table. 'And now you can all tell me what really happened yesterday.'

Over buttered scones, cakes and biscuits, they relived the battle of the playground.

'That's fine,' said Mary's mum. 'But what punishment are these two brave souls going to get for fighting and for leaving school early?'

'Detention, extra work and a ticking off,' the four of them chanted, and she laughed.

It was a happy group that broke up later that evening.

'See you Monday!' Mary called out as she watched the three pedal away along the rough track.

David whistled merrily as they went, but Debbie's head was buzzing with questions that had to be asked.

'How come you know them?' she began.

'Mary's mum works for my dad.'

'In the pub?'

'That's right. She does evenings,' David told them. 'That's why they've got that dog to look after Mary. He's a super dog. He comes down this track every day to meet her after school.'

'Can't her mum work in the day?'

'She does,' replied David. 'She goes over to the farmhouse and does the cleaning and washing. But she needs the extra money, see.'

'What about Mary's dad, then?'

'If I tell you, you must promise not to say anything to anyone,' said David. 'Her mum's afraid she might have a bad time at school.'

Debbie and Clare promised faithfully.

'He's in prison,' said David. 'He's in the county gaol. They came here to live so as to be near him. They go and visit him every Sunday.'

'What did he do?'

'He stole money,' David explained. 'He got laid off work on a building site up London way. He couldn't get another job and he couldn't pay the rent either, so he did a bit of breaking and entering and got caught. Mary and her mum got chucked out of their home, so my dad got the farmer to let them move into the caravan.'

'But how did your dad get involved?' They were still puzzled.

'It's family!' David grinned. 'Mary's dad is his brother.'

Much later that evening as the two girls reached Debbie's house they stopped by the gate.

'It just shows, you can't always tell what a person is really like, can you?' said Debbie. 'Mary's great and so is her mum.'

'Yes, and David, too,' grinned Clare.

'Snap of the Chain'

ZOE GLEADHALL (AGED 14)

These are the trees which fill the forests
All in the world that God made.

These are the trees which fill the forests
That form fossil fuel
All in the world that God made.

These are the trees which fill the forests
That form fossil fuel
That powers the boilers
All in the world that man made.

These are the trees which fill the forests
That form fossil fuel
That powers the boilers
That exude the fumes
All in the world that man made.

These are the trees which fill the forests
That form fossil fuel
That powers the boilers
That exude the fumes
That produce acid rain
All in the world that man made.

'Snap of the Chain'

These are the trees which fill the forests
That form fossil fuel
That powers the boilers
That exude the fumes
That produce acid rain
That kills the forests
All in the world that God made.

Zilya's Secret Plan

ULRICH SCHAFFER

Zilya lives in a beautiful valley. There are green meadows in the
valley, and tall trees. There are flowers and butterflies – and a river as
blue as the sky. All around the valley are high mountains. There is
snow on the mountains all the year round. When God made the
world, Zilya thought, he must have wanted to make this valley
especially beautiful.

Zilya likes to build little boats and float them down the river. She
loves her beautiful valley very much.

One day, when she was watching her boats, she saw some people
by the river. They were throwing all their empty bottles and cans into
the water. Then they got into their car and started off in a rush. The
wheels spun, crushing and chewing up the grass.

'Poor, poor grass!' said Zilya, stroking it gently. She was very sad to
see the meadow grass hurt.

A few days later, more people came. They carved their names into
the bark of a white birch. They laughed as they cut the tree – and did
not hear the white birch scream. But Zilya heard.

'Little birch, don't cry, don't cry,' she said when the people had
gone. 'Your bark will heal.' As soon as the birch heard Zilya's voice it
stopped shivering and began to feel better.

Next day, Zilya saw a family having a picnic in the woods near her
house. The children had slings. They shot at the trees, at the flowers,
at the insects. A big, blue-black raven flew over their heads. They
shot at that, and killed it. The raven dropped to the ground. The
children just laughed and went on playing. Zilya couldn't believe her
eyes. How could they?

Something had to be done.

Zilya went to the mayor of the village.

'People are spoiling our grass, hurting our trees and killing our
creatures,' she said.

But the mayor wasn't listening. 'Go away, little girl,' he said. 'Can't you see I'm busy?'

The months went by, and many things happened in the valley to make Zilya sad.

'If this goes on, our beautiful valley will be spoiled,' she said to herself. And that was when she thought of her secret plan.

She called her friends to the place where the river and the forest and the meadow all meet. The animals gathered round. The blades of grass bent forward. No one wanted to miss a word that Zilya said. Even the birds stopped chirping. And the rabbits pricked up their long ears.

Zilya told them her plan.

Next morning the people in the village got up, and looked out of their windows as usual. Strange. How quiet it was! They couldn't hear any birds.

'Where have all the birds gone? What's happening?' Zilya knew what was happening.

She had planned it. But she didn't say a word.

The day after that, all the wild animals were gone.

No squirrels were gathering food.

No rabbits hopped across the meadows.

There were no moles, no mice, no foxes, no badgers – anywhere.

On the third day all the insects had disappeared.

No buzzing flies.

No bugs, no beetles, no bees, no wasps.

No grasshoppers whirred in the meadow.

No butterflies fluttered from flower to flower.

No ants scurried to and fro.

And in the evening, no moths gathered around the light.

On the fourth day there was an even bigger surprise. When the people in the village looked out of their windows, there were no trees.

The poplars around the school were gone.

The big oak tree in the middle of the village, where the children loved to play, had disappeared.

So had the birches and willows, the maples and beeches.

Even the fir-trees on the mountains had gone.

The valley looked empty and bare.

That evening there was a meeting in the village.

'What's happening?' everyone asked. 'First the birds, then the wild animals and the insects – and now all the trees. Where have they gone? What *is* happening?'

The people were shouting by now. But no one knew the answer. They asked the mayor, but he didn't know, either.

Zilya was there. But when she tried to speak the grown-ups said, 'What are you doing here? This isn't a meeting for children.' And they sent her home.

On the fifth day the grass was gone. One of the people, who got up early, saw the last blades of grass disappearing. Only the bare earth remained, brown and black.

The cows walked around in surprise: there was nothing for them to eat.

Another meeting was called. Once again, Zilya went. This time she stepped right up to the mayor.

'Mr Mayor, I know what we must do.' But again he refused to listen.

'You here again?' he said – and rudely pushed her aside.

'If you don't listen,' Zilya called to him, 'something worse will happen tomorrow!' Then she put her hands behind her back and walked away. She didn't even turn round.

Next day, it was true, something worse *had* happened.

The river was empty.

There was no water for the cows, or the people, to drink.

Everyone could see the ugly, rusty tins and rubbish sticking out of the mud at the bottom of the river.

At midday the sun was hot and the river began to smell. It seemed as if the whole valley was dying.

Now the valley was really dead. Everything was drab and grey. Sadly the people thought about their beautiful valley.

Someone said: 'It seems as if God is taking back all the lovely things he made and gave us.'

At last the people began to understand how much they needed the birds, the animals, the insects, the trees, the grass – and the sparkling, rushing, singing river.

When the mayor saw the dried-up river he remembered what Zilya had said.

'Zilya,' he said, 'tell me how you knew that something worse would happen.'

'It was all part of the plan,' Zilya said. And she told the mayor the whole story. She told him how the creatures of the valley were afraid, because no one took care of them. She told him how they had planned to leave, to show people just what the valley would be like without them.

Then the mayor called the village people together.

'We have to take better care of our valley,' he said. 'When God made the world, he put us in charge of it. He told us to take care of all his creatures. But we haven't done it. Zilya has shown us what our valley is like without all these things. We have to change. From now on, all the rubbish must be tidied up and taken away. We must protect the flowers and the animals. Anyone who hurts them will be punished. And no one is allowed to cut down trees without special permission.'

He said a lot of other things, too. Then he turned to Zilya: 'Please tell all your friends to come back now. We love them and we promise to take better care of them.'

Zilya knew he really meant it. She was very happy.

Next morning Zilya packed a knapsack and set off into the mountains where all her friends were hiding.

When they saw her they came out to meet her.

'You can all come back again,' she said. 'The plan has worked. The people have changed. They have remembered how God told them to take care of you. They know they can't live without you.'

When they heard this they were all very happy, for they knew they belonged to the valley. They began to move down the hillside, towards the village.

The birds flew overhead, singing their very best songs.

The river began to flow again, and the fish leaped.

The rabbits and the foxes and all the other animals hopped and skipped and jumped in the air for joy.

The green grass grew again in the valley.

The trees marched like an army. As the wind rushed through their branches, Zilya could hear the happy chatter of the leaves.

Right across the village street was a banner: WELCOME HOME! The village had its best party ever. Everyone joined in, but Zilya was the most important guest. Zilya had saved the valley, and everyone knew it.

The Lost Princess

From *The Snow Goose*

PAUL GALLICO

The Snow Goose is a sad and beautiful story of England in war-time. Lonely Philip Rhayader lives in an abandoned lighthouse on the east coast. He is disabled, and people are frightened of him. But he's a painter who specially loves the wild birds, and they love him.
So Frith brings him the injured snow goose which will play an important part in both their lives.

One November afternoon, three years after Rhayader had come to the Great Marsh, a child approached the lighthouse studio by means of the sea wall. In her arms she carried a burden.

She was no more than twelve, slender, dirty, nervous and timid as a bird, but beneath the grime as eerily beautiful as a marsh faery. She was pure Saxon, large-boned, fair, with a head to which her body was yet to grow, and deep-set, violet-coloured eyes.

She was desperately frightened of the ugly man she had come to see, for legend had already begun to gather about Rhayader, and the native wild-fowlers hated him for interfering with their sport.

But greater than her fear was the need of that which she bore. For locked in her child's heart was the knowledge, picked up somewhere in the swampland, that this ogre who lived in the lighthouse had magic that could heal injured things.

She had never seen Rhayader before and was close to fleeing in panic at the dark apparition that appeared at the studio door, drawn by her footsteps – the black head and beard, the sinister hump, and the crooked claw.

She stood there staring, poised like a disturbed marsh bird for instant flight.

But his voice was deep and kind when he spoke to her.

'What is it, child?'

She stood her ground, and then edged timidly forward. The thing she carried in her arms was a large white bird, and it was quite still. There were stains of blood on its whiteness and on her kirtle where she had held it to her.

The girl placed it in his arms. 'I found it, sir. It's hurted. Is it still alive?'

'Yes. Yes, I think so. Come in, child, come in.'

Rhayader went inside, bearing the bird, which he placed upon a table, where it moved feebly. Curiosity overcame fear. The girl followed and found herself in a room warmed by a coal fire, shining with many coloured pictures that covered the walls, and full of a strange but pleasant smell.

The bird fluttered. With his good hand Rhayader spread one of its immense white pinions. The end was beautifully tipped with black.

Rhayader looked and marvelled, and said: 'Child: where did you find it?'

'In t' marsh, sir, where fowlers had been. What – what is it, sir?'

'It's a snow goose from Canada. But how in all heaven came it here?'

The name seemed to mean nothing to the little girl. Her deep violet eyes, shining out of the dirt on her thin face, were fixed with concern on the injured bird.

She said: 'Can 'ee heal it, sir?'

'Yes, yes,' said Rhayader. 'We will try. Come, you shall help me.'

There were scissors and bandages and splints on a shelf, and he was marvellously deft, even with the crooked claw that managed to hold things.

He said: 'Ah, she has been shot, poor thing. Her leg is broken, and the wing tip! But not badly. See, we will clip her primaries, so that we can bandage it, but in the spring the feathers will grow and she will be able to fly again. We'll bandage it close to her body, so that she cannot move it until it has set, and then make a splint for the poor leg.'

Her fears forgotten, the child watched, fascinated, as he worked, and all the more so because while he fixed a fine splint to the shattered leg he told her the most wonderful story.

The bird was a young one, no more than a year old. She was born in a northern land far, far across the seas, a land belonging to England. Flying to the south to escape the snow and ice and bitter cold, a great storm had seized her and whirled and buffeted her about. It was a truly terrible storm, stronger than her great wings, stronger than anything. For days and nights it held her in its grip and there was nothing she could do but fly before it. When finally it had blown itself out and her sure instincts took her south again, she was over a different land and surrounded by strange birds that she had never seen before. At last, exhausted by her ordeal, she had sunk to rest in a friendly green marsh, only to be met by the blast from the hunter's gun.

'A bitter reception for a visiting princess,' concluded Rhayader. 'We will call her "*La Princesse Perdue*," the Lost Princess. And in a few days she will be feeling much better. See!' He reached into his pocket and produced a handful of grain. The snow goose opened its round yellow eyes and nibbled at it.

The child laughed with delight, and then suddenly caught her breath with alarm as the full import of where she was pressed in upon her, and without a word she turned and fled out of the door.

'Wait, wait!' cried Rhayader, and went to the entrance, where he stopped so that it framed his dark bulk. The girl was already fleeing down the sea wall, but she paused at his voice and looked back.

'What is your name, child?'

'Frith.'

'Eh?' said Rhayader. 'Fritha, I suppose. Where do you live?'

'Wi' t' fisherfolk at Wickaeldroth.' She gave the name the old Saxon pronunciation.

'Will you come back tomorrow, or the next day, to see how the Princess is getting along?'

She paused, and again Rhayader must have thought of the wild water birds caught motionless in that split second of alarm before they took to flight.

But her thin voice came back to him: 'Ay!'

And then she was gone, with her fair hair streaming out behind her.

The snow goose mended rapidly and by midwinter was already limping about the enclosure with the wild pink-footed geese with which it associated, rather than the barnacles, and had learned to come to be fed at Rhayader's call. And the child, Fritha, or Frith, was a frequent visitor. She had overcome her fear of Rhayader. Her imagination was captured by the presence of this strange white princess from a land far over the sea, a land that was all pink, as she knew from the map that Rhayader showed her, and on which they traced the stormy path of the lost bird from its home in

Canada to the Great Marsh of Essex.

Then one June morning a group of late pink-feet, fat and well fed from the winter at the lighthouse, answered the stronger call of the breeding grounds and rose lazily, climbing into the sky in ever widening circles. With them, her white body and black-tipped pinions shining in the spring sun, was the snow goose. It so happened that Frith was at the lighthouse. Her cry brought Rhayader running from the studio.

'Look! Look! The Princess! Be she going away?'

Rhayader stared into the sky at the climbing specks.

'Ay,' he said, unconsciously dropping into her manner of speech. 'The Princess is going home. Listen! She is bidding us farewell.'

Out of the clear sky came the mournful barking of the pink-feet, and above it the higher, clearer note of the snow goose. The specks drifted northward, formed into a tiny v, diminished, and vanished.

With the departure of the snow goose ended the visits of Frith to the lighthouse. Rhayader learned all over again the meaning of the word 'loneliness.'

That summer, out of his memory, he painted a picture of a slender, grime-covered child, her fair hair blown by a November storm, who bore in her arms a wounded white bird.

In mid-October the miracle occurred. Rhayader was in his enclosure, feeding his birds. A grey north-east wind was blowing and the land was sighing beneath the incoming tide. Above the sea and the wind noises he heard a clear, high note. He turned his eyes upward to the evening sky in time to see first an infinite speck, then a black-and-white pinioned dream that circled the lighthouse once, and finally a reality that dropped to earth in the pen and came waddling forward importantly to be fed, as though she had never been away. It was the snow goose. There was no mistaking her. Tears of joy came to Rhayader's eyes. Where had she been? Surely not home to Canada. No, she must have summered in Greenland or Spitzbergen with the pink feet. She had remembered and had returned.

When next Rhayader went into Chelmbury for supplies, he left a message with the postmistress – one that must have caused her much bewilderment. He said: 'Tell Frith, who lives with the fisherfolk at Wickaeldroth, that the Lost Princess has returned.'

Angel Train

NAN HUNT

It was headline news…
BOY SNATCHED FROM BED

Who was he?
Where from?
Why?
Rich kid? Poor kid?
'Poor *kid*!' they all said when they heard it.
The blue off-roader belonging to a Frontier Services Patrol Padre was stolen – of course. The boy did not know that. He did not need to know. He had been taken from his bed. No one told him why. No one told him anything.
'Just shut up! Sit still. Or get hurt.'
He knew what to do. He did not speak. He sat as still as he could. The sleeves of his pyjamas were tied behind his back. His hands too.

It was dark. It had been dark for a long time. The tyres hummed on the bitumen. *Pow-wer Pow-wer Pow-wer.*
The boy slept; woke up. All the sounds were the same. He slept again. He did not hear when the man talked on his two-way radio. 'What? The *wrong boy*?' The curses, the repeated instructions.

Slow, gears, bumps, a different surface under the tyres, the jerk of the seat-belt as the vehicle stopped.
The boy woke up, startled.
'You wait here. You can watch the trains; listen to the CD. Be good.'
A door slammed. The boy heard feet on dry earth. A cough. Then silence except for the engine.
The CD came to life. There was singing. Hymns: old words, not

132

what he was used to. An organ, not a guitar.
> *'with his angel train'*

Train, yes! Train!

'You can watch the trains,' the man had said.

Why did an angel need a train? Did it have tired wings? Was it for holidays? A train full of angels? He knew kids who had been on a train, a holiday train, going far away. Or had the angel flown into power lines?

ZAP!

The CD ran down into silence. The boy moved to ease a numb cheek. He was in the middle of the back seat, hemmed in by boxes. How long had the man been gone?

He strained to hear if a train was coming, holding his breath. No.

The blue off-roader sat alone. The Australian sky was blue too. Not the same blue. The sun was red. The earth, too, was red. Not the same red as the sun. The rails were dull, with silver top where the wheels kept them shiny. The metal of the track was stained. Cement sleepers had sand blown over them and off them. The wind decided how and when.

The boy waited. The land waited. At home, the boy's family waited.

The news again:
> *NO SIGN OF MISSING BOY*

The boy's dog fretted.

Search parties looked all over, but not off the road where the boy was. Not in the red dirt under the blue sky with the hot sun over all.

He heard the train coming. Lots of wheels. Lots and lots and lots of wheels. *kerPUNK kerPUNK kerPUNK kerPUNK.* A heavy load from the sound of it, the boy said to himself. A long, long train. Ore? Going to the coast then, from the mine. Was the man watching the train? Had he been waiting for it? He had been gone a long time.

The train driver saw the off-roader beside the line. No one around. The sun bounced on the body of it. It did not look damaged. He did not see the boy in the back, but made a note of the time and place, and talked into his two-way radio.

The boy tried to count. Wheels. Trucks. The train did not stop. He was thirsty. Hot. The air-conditioning had gone off when the engine stopped. The temperature climbed with the sun.

The man. What was the man doing? Had he wandered off, lost? He tried to remember. In the dark when the man went away. After he'd gone there had been a noise, far off. The boy did not know what made the noise. Not a train. He wished he had taken more notice. Then it had not mattered, he was listening to the singing. Now it did.

He tried to collect spit in his mouth to swallow. It was so hot in the seat. He could not get his arms free. It exhausted him. And he had to do as he was told. Shut up. Sit still.

Or did he?

He tried to slide under the seat-belt. He was stuck. He was afraid. He was sure the man did not mean to come back. Ever. 'You can watch the trains.' The man was mean and cruel.

The boy lay panting. He knew he could die under the hot sun if nobody came. It made him angry. 'I will *not* die!' he shouted. Nobody heard.

Nobody?

Suddenly the singing was in his head.
'coming with his angel train'
Hope ran into his mind from his heart. Coming! The Angel Train *would* come!

Shut up. Sit still. Wait here.

His dog Penny was good at waiting. He almost felt her soft wet tongue on his hand.

His head drooped to one side. Were feathers soft? Angel wings – downy or made of silver? Sweat stained his clothes. Water was soft. No, he had been in rain that bit and stung. *Angel Train.* There had been a train. An ore train. The Angel Train had to be next.

The boy's mind drifted as the sun moved across the sky. He lost all sense of time.

The train approached slowly. When it reached the place where the blue off-roader sat on the red earth, the driver blew the whistle. Brakes squealed.

The boy jerked in his seat.

The train clanked to a stop.

He had known all along that it would come. The Angel Train!

The one that was coming! Now it had come. He would feel the feathers, surely?

He smelled the sweat, heard the kind voice after the first angry exclamation, felt the rough hands freeing him, lifting him carefully and cradling him against a shoulder. His cheek fell against the angel's face. It was prickly. 'Silver,' the boy said, putting his hand up to feel. 'Not feathers.'
'Eh?' said the man. 'What's that?'

The train was fast. The boy, washed, and given a drink, was happy. He was on the Angel Train, and soon, soon he would be home and safe.
'I'm alive!' he shouted. 'I didn't die! The Angel Train *did* come!'

The news flashed across the nation:
BLIND BOY SURVIVES ORDEAL

'He's Got the Whole World in his Hands'

SPIRITUAL

He's got the whole world in his hands;
He's got the whole world in his hands.

He's got the little bitty baby in his hands;
He's got the whole world in his hands.

He's got the trees and the flowers in his hands;
He's got the whole world in his hands.

He's got the wind and the rain in his hands;
He's got the whole world in his hands.

He's got the seas and the rivers in his hands;
He's got the whole world in his hands.

He's got you and me, brother, in his hands;
He's got you and me, sister, in his hands.

He's got the whole world in his hands!

6
To the Rescue!

People and animals – we all share Planet Earth.
We need each other and can help one another, too.
That's why I've put these stories together.
The first two are about Noah and the ark. God's big rescue
story, told from the Bible, is followed by an imaginative and
very funny account of Mr Noah's problems. Some of these
stories, like *Yamacuchi's Harvest* from Japan, are about
rescuing people. In others, like *The Eyrie* and *Kippy Koala* –
an exciting Australian story for younger readers – it's animals
to the rescue.

The Flood – and a Rainbow

From *My Own Book of Bible Stories*

PAT ALEXANDER

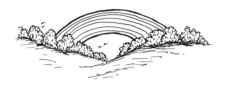

This story comes from the first book of the Bible,
Genesis, chapters 6–9.

Adam and Eve left the garden of Eden. Children were born and grew
up. Old people died – as God had said. Many years went by, and
there were many people in God's world. But they fought and stole.
They were cruel and unkind. They told lies. They never thought
about God or listened to him. When God saw what was happening,
how the people were spoiling his world, he was sad. He knew he
would have to start all over again.

But there was one man, Noah, who loved God and listened to
him, and did as God said.

So God said to him, 'Noah, you must build a strong boat – a big
one with room for all your family, and for two of every kind of
animal. Very soon I shall send rain and there will be a great flood.
Every creature on earth will drown – except you and your family and
the birds and animals. You will be safe, if you do as I say.'

Noah did as God said. Everyone laughed when they saw him.
'A boat? Here? Miles from the sea?' But Noah took no notice. He just
did as God said.

At last the boat was ready.

'In seven days the rain will come,' God said. 'Take two of every
kind of bird and animal and settle them inside. And take plenty of
food.'

Noah did as God told him.

Last of all he and his family went on board.

People were still laughing when the first black rain-cloud moved
across the sky. Big drops of rain bounced down on the hard dry
earth. Everyone ran indoors.

Lightning flashed. Thunder crashed. Little puddles became big puddles. Big puddles became lakes. And the lakes became a wide rising sea.

The flood lifted Noah's boat and carried it high above the houses and fields. High above the woods and hills. High above the highest mountain. Soon there was no dry ground left. The flood covered everything. No one, nothing, was left alive – except on Noah's boat. God kept Noah, and his family, and all the birds and animals safe.

For forty days it rained. Then the rain stopped and God sent a dry wind. Slowly, slowly the water began to go down.

Bump! The boat touched land. It was resting on the side of a mountain. But there was still a sea of water all around. On board, everyone began to get irritable. They were so tired of being shut up. How much longer?

Noah sent out a dove. She flew around and came back. The trees were still under water. Seven days later Noah sent her out again. This time she came back with a fresh green leaf in her beak. Everyone cheered: 'Hurray! Not long now.'

At last God spoke to Noah. 'It's time to leave,' he said. They took off the cover and opened the door. The muddy water had gone. The sun shone. The world looked green and new. There was a great rush to get out. The animals jumped for joy and the birds all sang at once. As for Noah and his family, 'Thank you, oh thank you, God,' they said. It was so good to feel the firm ground under their feet and smell the flowers.

'Look up at the sky,' God said to Noah. And there overhead was a glorious rainbow.

'I will never again send a flood to destroy the world,' God said. 'The rainbow in the sky will remind me of my promise.'

Noah's Tale

From *More Tales from the Ark*

AVRIL ROWLANDS

Mr Noah was a worried man. He had been ever since God had dropped his bombshell and turned Mr Noah's life upside down.

'I am afraid,' God had said to Mr Noah, 'that I shall have to destroy the world and every living creature, for it has become an evil place. But I shall save you, Mr Noah, and your wife and sons and their wives. And I shall save two of all the living creatures in the world.'

God told Mr Noah to build a wooden ark, which was like a large boat, so that when he sent a flood to cover the earth, Mr Noah, his family and the animals would be saved.

'And you, Mr Noah, will look after the animals for me, for they are all important. I'm relying on you to keep them alive.'

Mr Noah was sad at the thought of the world being destroyed and worried at the job God had given him to do. He pleaded with God.

'I'm very grateful, God, please believe me, but I don't think I'm the right person. I've never kept any animals apart from two cats, and I've only got them to keep the mice down. I don't even really like animals. I'm sure you could choose someone better than me.'

But God wanted Mr Noah.

Mr Noah tried again. 'I'm not a very good organizer, God, and you'll need a good organizer for this trip. I get muddled, you see.'

But God did not reply. Besides, he had every faith in Mr Noah.

'It's not as if I'm a young man,' Mr Noah told his wife that night. 'God should have chosen a younger, better man for the job.' (Mr Noah was six hundred years old at the time.)

'A younger one maybe,' said his wife, 'but there's not a better one. And God chose *you* for the job, so do try and get some sleep.'

But sleep would not come to Mr Noah that night. He tossed and turned and worried. At last he sat bolt upright.

'What on earth do aardvarks eat?' he demanded. But his wife was snoring gently by his side and did not reply.

Mr Noah had had little sleep since then. As the days passed, his worries grew.

'Ouch!' he cried, as he hit his thumb with a hammer for the third time.

'Look, Father,' said his eldest son Shem, 'why don't you go and welcome the animals and leave building the ark to us?'

His other sons, Ham and Japheth, nodded in agreement.

'I'm sure you've got plenty of other work to do,' Shem added tactfully.

'And you know you're not much good at carpentry,' Ham said bluntly.

Mr Noah looked stubborn. 'God told *me* to build the ark,' he said.

Shem, Ham and Japheth looked at each other, then carried on with the building. But after a few minutes...

'Owwh!' cried Mr Noah, as he hit his sore thumb for a fourth time.

'Please, Father...' said Shem.

Just then Mrs Noah called from the house.

'Noah, will you come? Two flamingos have arrived and say they must speak to you. They seem a bit upset.'

Mr Noah climbed down from the ark. He was really quite pleased to have an excuse to go, and his sons were equally pleased to be rid of him.

'Now we can get on faster,' said Ham.

Mr Noah did not return to the ark. After he had talked to the flamingos, the chimpanzees had to be chased off his grapevines. Then the beavers arrived and began building a dam across the stream which provided water for Mr Noah's farm. The emus turned their noses up at the sleeping arrangements and one of the polar bears fainted with the heat. Mr Noah was kept very busy. There was so much to do and so little time.

'Can't you get some of the animals to give you a hand?' his wife asked, as they ate their evening meal. 'Those nice elephants offered to help the boys with the building, and even the monkeys said they'd swing down and pick up the tools that got dropped – not that I trust them that much. Very sarcastic they were.'

'The beavers want to help, too,' said Japheth.

'I can't have help,' Mr Noah replied. 'God gave *me* the job and I must do it by myself.'

'But you're not building the ark by yourself,' his wife pointed out. 'Our sons are helping.'

'Yes,' said Mr Noah, frowning. 'But perhaps I should have tried.'

'The ark would sink,' Ham said.

'Don't be so rude to your father!' said his mother sharply, but Mr Noah was not even listening.

How could he make sure that two of every animal, insect and bird were on board at the right time? Say he missed one or two? God might never forgive him. Word must already have got around, for animals were beginning to arrive, turning up at Mr Noah's farmhouse at all hours of the day and night. It was a problem knowing where to put them and how to feed them, and the two chimpanzees could not be stopped from stripping the grapes from his vineyards.

Food was another problem. How was he to get all the food required for so many animals? Mr Noah spent hours making lists of what the animals, insects and birds ate. It made depressing reading, for many of them just ate each other.

Then there was the building of the ark itself, which kept being
held up as Mr Noah was too busy to supervise the work.

Worries piled up along with the lists in Mr Noah's office. He grew
short-tempered and his sons and their wives and even Mrs Noah
began to avoid him. And as the day for boarding the ark drew nearer,
Mr Noah began to panic.

'It'll never be ready on time,' he thought, and hit his thumb and
fingers as he tried to work faster.

'The food'll never arrive in time,' he thought, and sent out
messages far and wide.

And one dreadful afternoon when the beavers successfully
dammed his stream and all the water to his farm dried up, and his
vineyards – long since stripped of grapes – were finally trampled
down by the hippos and the elephants, Mr Noah despaired.

He stopped doing any work and sat in the wreckage of his once
beautiful farm. Sadly he thought of his past life, remembering how
he had enjoyed watching his grapes grow round and fat under the
summer sun. Although he had complained about the hard work, he
had been content with his life. His eyes misted over and two fat tears
fell on the long list he held in his hand. He was too old for change
and it was all very frightening.

'I can't do it,' he thought, as he caught sight of the chimpanzees
scratching themselves for fleas. 'Should two fleas be taken on the
ark?' he wondered. God had not said anything about fleas.

He put his head in his hands and groaned. 'I can't do it.'

Then he jumped to his feet and began to pace up and down.

'I can't, I *can't*, I CAN'T DO IT! God will have to find someone else.
It's not too late.'

'Noah.'

It was God speaking, but Mr Noah did not hear him at first; he
was too upset.

'Noah, listen to me.'

'Oh, God, is that you?' Mr Noah said, words falling over
themselves in his panic. 'Where have you been? I've been so upset
and so worried and got into such a state. I don't want to leave,
I can't leave, and I can't do the job you've given me. I don't want to
die in the flood, but this is too much for an old man. Anyway, I don't
like animals – you should see the way some of them behave! Please,
God, find someone else.'

'Noah,' said God patiently. 'Stop talking, sit down and be quiet for a moment.'

Mr Noah did what God said and immediately began to feel a bit better.

'Now then, are you listening?'

'Yes, God,' said Mr Noah.

'Good. I've been wanting to help you for a long time, but you haven't given me the chance.'

'Haven't I?'

'No. You've been too busy trying to do everything yourself.'

'Have I?'

'Yes.'

'Oh,' said Mr Noah. 'I thought that was what you wanted.'

'You should have asked me, Noah,' said God.

'You haven't been around much lately,' Mr Noah grumbled. Then he felt ashamed. 'I expect you've been too busy.'

'I'm never too busy to help you,' said God. 'As long as you trust me, everything will turn out well.'

'Yes, God,' said Mr Noah.

'*Do* you trust me?' God asked, and it seemed to Mr Noah, as he sat in the sun among his ruined vineyards, that this was the most important question he had ever been asked. He thought back over his long life, remembering how, even as a child, he had always taken his problems to God. And God had never let him down, he thought. Not once. It was a long time before he spoke.

'Yes,' he said at last. 'Yes, God, I do trust you.'

'Well then,' said God. 'There's nothing for you to worry about.'

Mr Noah sat for a while longer, enjoying a sense of peace he had not known for a long time. Then he went back to his house and told his wife and sons that he was sorry for having been so bad-tempered. Everyone felt so much better that they worked even harder. Some of the animals helped, and soon the ark was ready.

And if Mr Noah still had worries, which he had – especially when he saw some of the more ferocious animals arrive on his farm – and if his stomach felt churned up at the thought of the future, which it did – many times a day – no one knew about it, except God. And God, Mr Noah knew, would help him with whatever lay ahead.

The Cat, the Monk and the Prince

From *Pangur Bán, the White Cat*

FAY SAMPSON

The white cat, Pangur Bán, was a killer. He crouched and waited.

There was definitely a mouse in the hole. He could see two bright, black eyes watching from the darkness.

The cat's white claws were tucked out of sight beneath him, but he was not resting. He lay low and still on the floor, but he was not asleep. Under his half-closed eyelids a narrow line of green showed, pierced by a black slit. He was watching. Every muscle was stretched tight, like a bent bow-string, an instrument of death.

'Don't move,' said Niall the monk, 'or I'll murder you.'

Pangur Bán did not answer, though he could talk very well when he wanted to.

Behind him, in the dusty sunlight, the long room was full of murmuring sound. Monks and nuns were bending over books, copying. As they traced the words, they said them aloud, so that they hummed over the painted pages, like brown bees in a meadow of flowers.

Where the open door gave on the sea, and the light fell brightest, young Niall sat painting the great title page of his Gospel. Three years he had been working on it, and there was no artist like him in all Erin. He was a giant of a man, an oak tree. But his strong brown hands could trace patterns as delicate as a spider weaving a cobweb on an April morning, and then paint them with all the splendour of the hills in autumn.

The calfskin page in front of him was stabbed with compass points. Red ink-dots, like drops of blood, traced the pattern. Ribbons of purple and blue twined between them, coiling, curling, circling. Knots of gold ended alarmingly in serpents' heads. And beyond their scarlet tongues, silver chariot wheels spun and spiralled upwards, till the whole rich carpet of the page became a letter p, flanked by astonished angels.

Now only one little empty space was left on the ivory-white

vellum. In less than an hour it would all be finished. Niall flexed his tired hands and looked up. His gaze fixed on Pangur, and he dipped his pen carefully into the scarlet paint. In the last corner of the page he began to outline with tiny red dots the shape of a white, crouching cat.

And the mouse came out of its hole.

Pangur Bán sprang.

With a squeal, the mouse was away. Under benches, under tables, under desks, to the far, dark, dusty end of the room. And Pangur Bán went after it, claws bared. Over the sandals of the monks, under the skirts of the nuns. The sound of their reading turned to shrieks of alarm.

The mouse reached the wall. In a panic it turned and swarmed up the white robe of the nearest nun onto her desk.

Pangur Bán whirled round, white feet in the black dust, and tore after it. Now they were flying back down the room over the table-tops. Dirty paw-prints on every clean white page. Claws tearing the painted words as he sprang. Pots of ink flying through the air. Shouts, cries, anger.

The mouse made a last leap for the sunlit doorway. Pangur Bán pounced onto Niall's desk. The pot of paint flew from the monk's hand, tipped over the all-but-finished page and rolled to the edge of the table. A pool of scarlet flowed out of it and began to drip, drip, drip onto the floor.

Pangur leaped after the mouse.

And Niall blocked the doorway. He was in a towering fury. He seized a stool by one leg, like a club. As Pangur skidded to a halt, Niall raised it above his head. Pangur sprang sideways. The blow smashed on to the floor. It would have split his skull.

'Help!' cried Pangur. 'Save me!'

Again Niall raised the stool.

'You murdering vermin! Look what you've done to my Gospel! Three years' work you've ruined. I'll dash your brains out for this!'

Pangur cowered.

'No!' cried a brave voice behind him.

Martin pushed in front of Niall. He was the youngest of all the monks, newly-come. A prince, who could have been king when his father Kernac died. But he worked in the kitchen. At night he fed Pangur with bread and milk, then held him purring on his knee.

Now he was as white as the milk itself, and not a quarter the size of Niall.

But, 'No, Niall!' he cried again. 'Don't hit him!'

'Out of my way!' roared Niall.

The stool crashed down again. And Martin threw himself under it, shielding Pangur.

He went down like a felled ash tree and lay in a heap on the floor. He was whiter than ever. Blood was trickling down the side of his face. The shouting was suddenly still.

'Martin!' cried Niall, kneeling down beside him. 'Martin! I didn't mean to! Not you!'

Pangur Bán crawled back into the shadows under the table and hid behind the skirts of the nuns.

Martin lay very still. The trickle of blood faltered and stopped. Behind him, the scarlet paint was still dripping off the table. Plop. Plop. Plop. It was the only sound in the long room.

The old nun Ita came forward. She rubbed a pewter paint pot against her sleeve. She held the shining metal to Martin's mouth. When she took it away, there was not a cloud of breath upon it. She looked at Niall and her face wrinkled in grief.

Donal the monk knelt down and felt for Martin's heart. No one spoke. At last he took his hand away and looked at Niall. They were all looking at Niall. And then they looked at Pangur.

'Martin?' mewed the cat.

'He's dead,' said Donal.

And there was only the sound of the waves swinging against the cliff. The monks and the nuns were all looking at Niall and Pangur.

Outside the door, the mouse scampered away in the sunshine. Safe.

Drusticc the Abbess stood on the beach, slender and white-robed on the white sand. She was young, loved and feared. They had buried Martin that morning, under the sea-pinks on the cliff.

'Now go!' she cried, her voice strong as the herring-gull's.

Niall knelt before her on the beach.

'But I didn't mean to kill him! I loved the lad. It wasn't my fault! It was that devil of a cat!'

Over his head her voice stormed. 'Of course it was your fault! Was it Pangur's hand that lifted the stool? Was it Pangur's arm that held it over your head? Was it Pangur's shoulders that brought it crashing down on Martin's skull? How could you do it, Niall? Martin, whom all of us loved. Martin, who never did you any wrong. How can you say it was the cat?'

'But he spilt the paint over my beautiful Gospel! He tore the page! He trampled his filthy footprints over everything!'

Pangur shrank further under the boat where he was crouching. There were no shadows dark enough to hide a white cat. He knew that it was true. Martin had died for him. He saw it in the faces of everyone he met. If they had not been monks and nuns they would have kicked him as he passed. No one fed him bread and milk now. No hand reached down to stroke his head.

Two monks came staggering down the beach. One carried a sack. The other had a cask on his shoulder.

'Go!' cried Drusticc in a ringing voice. 'Here is food and water. Go, until a year and a day have passed, and the spring has come to Erin again. And hear the penance that I lay upon the pair of you for the blood you have spilt.'

Pangur pricked up his ears and listened. Over his head was the swish, swish, swish of a brush. Enoch, the convent's fisherman, had been building the leather curragh all winter. Bending the wood, sewing the ox-hides, stepping the mast, cutting the sails. It was almost finished. Now he was painting it with hot sheep's grease to make it waterproof.

'You shall take a boat and go wherever the wind of God shall carry you. And wherever you go, you shall redeem with the lives of others the blood you have spilt; one life for every drop.'

The Old Woman and the Bear

An Inuit Tale

RETOLD BY JEAN WATSON

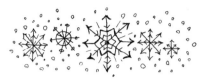

This is a tale from the frozen north, where the Inuit live. They are not very tall and they have small hands and feet. But they are strong. And they need to be, for they live by hunting wild creatures like bears and whales, seals and sea lions.

Once there was an old Inuit woman. She had no man to hunt for her, because her husband had died. But the people in her settlement were kind and brought her fish or meat after each day's hunting. All the same, she was sad and lonely, for she had nothing of her own to love.

One day, in the month of ice-beginning-to-form, the Inuit hunters brought back something quite different to the old woman. It was a tiny white bear cub, half dead from cold and hunger. The old woman took him from the men and, after they had gone, walked round the igloo, cradling the little white creature in her arms and singing softly to him. But still he lay stiff and cold against her heart. So she placed him gently on her drying frame. There the little creature lay, lapped by the warm air which rose from the fire in the middle of her igloo.

The old woman took her sharp ulo-knife and cut off a piece of whale's blubber. She put this in a dish and held it over the fire until the frozen flesh had turned into a thick soup. By this time the cub had opened his eyes, so she coaxed him into lifting his head and drinking some of the rich, warm liquid.

Afterwards, she waited and watched. At last, he began to move and look around. Then she took him out of the frame and set him gently down on the floor. Before long, he was frisking and gambolling about in the way all young things do when they are happy. Watching him, the old woman felt happy too. For now at last she had something of her own to love.

And how she loved that bear! In the days, weeks and months that followed, they played and worked and ate together. The old woman

149

even talked to him and he would sniff as though he understood. Sometimes the hunters in her settlement would come to visit them and to play wrestling games with the lively, friendly little cub. So the igloo would echo to the sounds of fun and laughter.

Time passed and the cub grew and grew until he was a full-grown bear. Then the hunters asked the old woman to let them take him on their hunting trips.

She did not want to let the bear go. But she knew how much he would enjoy the expeditions, so she agreed. And the bear did indeed love hunting with the men and was soon a very skilled hunter. He would crouch patiently beside the ice-holes, waiting for the whiskery faces of the seals to pop up. And as soon as they did, he would pounce like white lightning.

Now the old woman never went hungry. Often, she was so well supplied with whale blubber and seal meat that she was able to give away food to others. Only one thing troubled her. What if her bear should meet strangers from other settlements who did not know him and might attack him?

'I must make him a collar,' thought the old woman. 'So that anyone seeing him will know that he is not a wild bear.'

News of the friendly collared bear spread quickly from settlement to settlement. Soon everyone for miles around knew about him. And all who met him loved him and were kind to him. So the old woman stopped worrying and was happy again.

But there was one hunter who heard about the bear and thought, 'Our people have always hunted and killed bears, and that's the way things should continue. If ever I see this collared bear, I will certainly hunt and kill him, just as I would any other of his kind.'

One day, during a hunting trip, he and his fellow-hunters did indeed see the bear. At once they laid down their weapons and ran to greet him. But he, instead, raised his spear and charged at the creature. Terrified and bewildered, for he had never before been treated in this way, the bear turned and fled. The hunter pursued him, while his companions watched aghast, until the pair were out of sight.

That evening, the old woman sat in her igloo waiting for the return of the bear. He did not arrive at his usual time, and she began to feel afraid. As time passed, her fear grew and grew.

At last he came, and she greeted him with hugs and glad cries of welcome. But the bear did not respond in the usual way. He was trying to tell her something. He wanted her to follow him.

With a fast-beating heart, she went with him out of the igloo and across the snow. Before they had gone very far, the bear stopped. There at his feet lay the still figure of a hunter. The old woman could see that he was dead and that he was a stranger to her.

Dread filled her heart. For she knew at once what had happened and what might follow.

A hunter from another settlement had attacked the bear and been killed by the frightened creature in self-defence. But would the dead man's family and friends believe that? Probably not. And even if they did, they would want to avenge his death by killing the bear.

There was only one thing to do. She must send the bear back to the wild, back to his own kind. But how could she endure being separated from what she loved most? For several days she put off doing what she knew she must do. Then her love for the bear won the day. So long as he stayed with her, his life was in danger. She could delay the parting no longer.

With a breaking heart, she removed the collar from around the bear's neck and told him what had to happen. He gave a sorrowful sniff as if to say he understood but was sad too.

The old woman dipped one of her hands into a mixture of oil and soot. Then she put her arms around the bear and ran her fingers through his thick white fur until she had made a dark sooty patch in one of his sides.

'Now go,' she whispered brokenly. Slowly and sadly the bear obeyed and was soon lost to sight.

She never saw him again. But from time to time she heard hunters' tales of a wonderful bear: stronger, bigger and more skilful than any others of his kind, with a curious sooty black patch on one side of his body; a creature who never killed men no matter how fiercely they attacked him.

'That's my bear,' the old woman would think proudly. But she felt sad too for she never stopped missing her foster-child.

The Eyrie

From *Eagle Boy*

RODNEY BENNETT

*Stephan cannot speak and his club foot makes it hard
for him to walk. The superstitious villagers of Bletz think
Stephan brings them bad luck. They want to get rid of him.
So Stephan's father hides him in a cave.
Finding him there, an eagle claims Stephan for its own,
carrying him through the air to a nest high in the crags...*

Darkness crept over the mountains like a powerful liquid that has the property of dissolving massive rocks into insubstantial space. Only the rock beneath Stephan's body felt solid and secure, the rest was a black void.

For a long time, he lay huddled beneath the eagle's wing too frightened to move. A howling wind lashed the cliff, making their position seem so precarious that each time he felt the bird buffeted by the gale, he was sure they would be blown from the ledge and he would fall to the rocks below. But, like a brave mariner keeping watch, the eagle boldly faced the wind and flurries of snow, refusing to be dislodged from its perch.

As the hours passed, Stephan's terror slowly subsided. In spite of all that had happened, he began to feel grateful for the warmth of the eagle's body, for its strength and indomitable will. In the early hours of the morning he fell into a fitful sleep.

With the faint grey streaks of dawn the wind dropped and, for the first time, the eagle eased its cramped muscles and shook the snow from its feathers. It lifted its wing and looked with interest at the small figure huddled on the nest. Stephan stirred but did not wake. The bird gave an impatient squawk, folded its wing and hopped a pace away. Stephan woke with a start and, remembering where he was, gave a cry of alarm. The eagle preened its feathers, unmoved by the shouts of protest coming from the nest.

152

Shivering with the cold, with his knees clasped to his chest, Stephan was staring bleakly across the yawning abyss when a sudden miraculous transformation in the scene before him made him forget his wretchedness. The sun had just risen above the mountain peaks and was flooding the landscape with shafts of golden light. Below him, the mist hanging over the lower slopes was ablaze with every colour of the rainbow. It was like watching the creation of the world.

For several minutes, Stephan was transfixed by this elemental drama. Then, glancing at the eagle, he was met by another awesome sight. Caught in a shaft of light, with its wings folded round its body in a rich mantle of feathers and its proud neck crowned with a golden head, the great bird stood like an absolute monarch surveying its domain.

Sensing the boy looking at it, the eagle gave him an imperious stare. With an abrupt squawk, it leaped from the ledge and glided effortlessly into space. Stephan was on his feet at once shouting to it to return. The bird screeched short-temperedly but dropped a wing and circled back, flying so close to the boy that a wing tip brushed his face, toppling him back on the nest. Stay there! it screeched without pausing in its flight and with slow measured beats, it flew off across the mountains.

Earthbound, Stephan watched the bird until it was no more than a dark speck that finally disappeared in the far distance. He kicked aimlessly at a loose stone with his good foot and it fell silently into the abyss below. He felt very alone, very vulnerable – and very cold.

He was still huddled on the nest when some time later he heard beating wings overhead. He looked up to see the eagle swooping down towards him and, in a few moments, it landed expertly on the ledge. In its beak was the limp form of a dead vole. He watched the bird pin down the creature in its talons and rip open the fur with its beak. Then, it moved towards him with a morsel of flesh in its beak. Stephan recoiled in horror.

Puzzled, the bird moved closer, making odd little creaking sounds. Stephan cried out in protest, turning away and waving his arms. But the bird continued to advance until the meat was pressed against his face. In desperation, he scrambled to his feet and retreated along the ledge, pursued by the eagle.

Suddenly, as he took a step backwards, his foot landed on empty air. Wildly, he grabbed at the rocks. But they were already out of reach. In a flash, the eagle threw itself from the ledge and dived after him.

With talons already open it reached for the falling body, but only managed to rip the boy's clothes. The wings thrashed the air, trying to catch up with the boy who was plunging down like a stone. The talons grabbed again. And again. And finally secured themselves round the boy's waist. Now, the wings thrashed, fighting for control. But they could not check the falling dead weight, and eagle and boy dived together in a steeply curved arc, with the air screaming past their faces.

Still the rocks raced up to meet them as the eagle fought for mastery. At the lowest point in the arc, it braced its back and, with mighty beats of its wings, it pulled them back from the dive and into a swooping upward path. The sudden change of direction sent the blood rushing from Stephan's head to his stomach, and he almost lost consciousness.

It had all happened so quickly there had been no time to breathe, but as the climb continued and he was able to appreciate that he was out of danger, he gulped a mouthful of air and let it out in a cry that went echoing round the crags. It was nothing short of a miracle. One moment pulled by gravity to certain death; the next, hauled to safety by the colossal strength of the eagle.

The climb gradually levelled out and soon they were gliding round in a wide circle. Stephan trembled uncontrollably – an involuntary reaction to his fall – but this meant little to him compared to the joy he now felt of floating in the air, defying the pull of the earth. It was like being transported into the most perfect dream. It was all so smooth, quiet, graceful and effortless.

In his ecstasy, Stephan hardly noticed the eagle hovering over the ledge. But when he was dropped on the spiky nest, he was brought back to reality with an abrupt, painful bump.

The bird squawked disapprovingly and coolly shook its feathers into place. Stephan's face crumpled and he began to cry. Stop it! the bird rasped, as remote and stern as ever. The boy bit his lip as he tried to hold back his tears.

For a long time neither of them moved. Having rescued its captive the bird seemed to lose all interest in him. It was bewildering and frustrating for Stephan, who had been shown a world he never knew existed – a world in which he was no longer handicapped by the

weight of his clubbed foot and the uneven lengths of his legs, which made him sway and contort his body even when walking slowly. Those brief, heady moments of flight had been like chains falling from a prisoner. He knew now what it was like to be a free-floating spirit of the air – and nothing could equal that.

He glanced nervously at the eagle as it dozed in the pale sunlight, no longer a figure of majesty but an untidy mess of ruffled feathers. With the timidity of a child plucking up enough courage to speak to an august father, Stephan attempted a hesitant caw. The bird opened one eye and regarded him with a new interest. He cawed again, with more confidence, and the proud head slightly lifted as though deigning to accept the compliment.

Encouraged, Stephan sat up with a straight back and a brave tilt to his head. With legs crossed and arms folded, he quietly watched the shifting patterns of sunlight and shadow drifting across the mountain sides.

Kippy Koala and the Bushfire

WIN MORGAN

The sun blazed down out of a cloudless blue sky. A heat haze hung over the dusty, dry flats, where the deep river wandered, sluggish and grey. The bare roots of the river red-gums reached down towards the water like gnarled old fingers.

On a hillside away to the north of the river, tall gum trees grew, their trunks smooth and white and their arms stretched wide.

High in a fork of the tallest tree sat Kippy Koala, his thick grey overcoat with its white front neat and tidy and his brown button nose well-shined, happily dozing in the afternoon sun.

A sudden gust of hot wind made Kippy tighten his grip and raise his sleepy head. Clouds of dust were swirling and rising, tossing and tumbling ahead of the north wind as it swept over the flats towards the river.

White cockatoos flapped and screeched as they wheeled high on the hot gusts. A black crow sitting on a fence post croaked mournfully. Leaves and twigs scattered and circled about the tall trees. A sense of alarm prodded Kippy wide awake.

Backing out of his forked branch, Kippy scrambled to the ground. He stood still, sniffing a strange, new scent on the air.

I wonder what that is? said Kippy to himself.

There was a sound of scurrying feet. Kippy turned to see small bush animals hurrying by. They chattered anxiously to each other, scolding their babies and dragging them along as fast as their little legs could go.

The cavalcade of animals continued to push past Kippy, shouting at him, 'Move out of the way. Hurry! Hurry!'

Kippy suddenly felt very afraid. Where would he go? What would he do?

Big Red Kangaroo came bounding around the rocks. He saw Kippy standing at the foot of his tall tree, a bewildered look on his furry face, and spun to a halt.

Kippy can't run. He'll never escape the fire, Red thought. 'Come on, Kippy,' he said. 'I'll help you. Climb on my back and hold on tight!'

Leaping and bounding down the hillside, over the stumps and across the dry creek-bed, Big Red and Kippy soon caught up with the frightened bush animals. They were so tired, they stumbled and tripped. How could they possibly outrun the terrible fire?

Billows of smoke turned the sun into a red ball. The air was filled with burning leaves, driven furiously along by the rushing north wind.

Kippy clung onto Big Red's back for all his might, as they dashed for cover.

The sound of the flames racing in the treetops brought a great fear to the animals and they gathered together in alarm.

'The fire will catch us. We'll be burnt alive,' they cried. 'What can we do?'

'You're too slow,' said Wally Wallaby, impatiently. 'I'm not waiting for you. If I do, the fire will catch us *all*.' And he bounded off on his own, heading for the deep river flats.

'What about us?' the echidnas and possums and lizards all sobbed. 'Who can help us?'

'Now keep calm,' called Big Red. 'There must be some way out.'

The animals all turned to Big Red, waiting for his answer. But he only furrowed his brow, gazing anxiously at his bush friends.

'If we can find out which way the fire is headed, maybe we can find a safe place to shelter,' he said.

Suddenly Kippy spoke up. He couldn't run fast and he wasn't a leader, like Big Red. But there was something he could do better than any of the others.

'I have an idea.'

Quickly he chose a tall, straight tree and scrambled up, gripping with his sharp claws until he reached the top branches.

The north wind tossed the treetop this way and that, as Kippy anxiously searched for a place of safety. He looked back the way they had come and saw the flames racing over the hilltop.

We can't possibly outrun the fire, he thought. There must be somewhere we can shelter.

Looking up the valley, he saw the rocky outcrop by the dry creek-bed, where Uncle Wainwright Wombat lived. His hollow in the rocks was their only chance.

As Kippy hurried down the tree, the animals gathered around him.

'Well, what did you see?' they asked.

'The fire is racing straight towards us. Wally Wallaby was wrong. Not even the fastest of us could keep ahead of it,' Kippy answered. 'Our only chance is to get to Uncle Wainwright's before the flames get to us. That means going to the cave, not the river. Will you do as I say?'

Eyes wide with terror, they could only nod their heads and gather their babies, ready to make a dash down the rocky hillside across the face of the fire.

'Stay together and follow us,' called Kippy over the roar of the wind and the fire which raced through the treetops. 'This is the only way out!'

The billowing smoke cast an eerie orange light as it blotted out the burning sun. Hot white ash and burning leaves were driven into Kippy's eyes and fell on his grey, furry coat. The animals stumbled and cried.

'We should have gone with Wally Wallaby. Where are we going? We'll never make it.'

'You're leading us *towards* the fire, Kippy,' cried a ringtail possum.

'No, no. We'll be safe. But we have to cross its path first. Hurry! We must reach the cave before the flames catch us,' shouted Kippy.

'It is dangerous, but it's our only hope,' cried Big Red. 'We can't stay ahead of the fire any longer.'

They struggled and slipped on the rocky slopes, panting for breath in the searing heat.

Big Red and Kippy stumbled around the huge rocks in the dry creek-bed, leading them all to the shadowy opening of Uncle Wainwright Wombat's hollow in the hillside.

'Uncle, please let us in,' called Kippy. 'The fire is coming over the hills and we need shelter.'

Grumbling at being disturbed from his afternoon nap, Wainwright Wombat peered out at the odd gathering of bush animals outside his front door.

'Why, it's Kippy Koala! Come in, all of you. Don't be frightened. You'll be safe from the bushfire in here.'

The animals squeezed through the opening, pulling Big Red in with them. The roaring wind drove the fire through the treetops. It was so hot, they could hardly breathe. Smoke and flames billowed over the entrance, as the fire raced across the creek-bed.

At last the terrifying sound of the raging fire faded into the distance. Kippy Koala gazed sadly out across the blackened hillside where the tall gums, golden wattle and pink heath had once grown. He wiped the tears from his stinging eyes.

Proud trees lay shattered on the blackened earth. Smoke rose and drifted across the creek-bed. Ash and cinders covered the bare rocks. There was no sound now of the cockatoos or crow. A sad silence settled over the desolate bushland.

Turning away, Kippy said, 'Thank you for keeping us safe from the bushfire, Uncle Wainwright. We'd have died if you hadn't let us shelter here.'

Softly the animals whimpered, 'If only Wally Wallaby had listened, he would have been safe, too. He could run, but he couldn't climb trees to see what Kippy saw.'

'That's true,' replied Kippy. 'We are all good at different things. We all need each other. If we help one another now, one day – when the rains come – our beloved bush will come back to life and we shall be happy and safe again.'

Yamacuchi's Harvest

PEGGY HEWITT

Yamacuchi felt tired but very happy. It had been a hard day. From early morning until the sun went down everybody in the village had been working in the fields, gathering in the harvest before the hard winter weather began. All day the loaded carts had trundled backwards and forwards until everybody's barn was full; it had been a good harvest and they knew that nobody would go hungry in the village during the coming year. Yamacuchi was an old man, but there had been plenty of willing people to help him, and his barn too was full.

He heaved a sigh of contentment and looked round the village, perched on its cliff above the sea. He had lived there all his life and knew every single villager, even the newest baby, and he thought of them all as his family. But now the village was empty.

After all the hard work was finished everybody had changed into their party clothes and gone down to the beach for a celebration. They had tried to persuade him to go with them, pulling at his hands and laughing, but he had said he felt too tired and eventually they left him. But before they went they had brought a chair out of his house and put it where he could sit and watch the party on the beach, and they had put a burning torch in a holder by his side so that he didn't feel too much alone.

So now he sat, nodding drowsily in the twilight, delicious smells of roasting meat drifting up to him from the fires, mixing with the sounds of laughing and music. It had been a long time since he had been to a party, but he could still remember the fun he'd had, and how he could dance longer than anybody else – and faster – when he was a young man. With difficulty he opened his eyes to watch his friends on the beach again – then he stiffened in his chair, and his old hands clutched tightly at the chair arms.

Something very strange was happening to the sea.

It was running back off the sand towards the distant horizon, faster than any tide. Even as he watched, the expanse of sand became wider and wider, gleaming wetly, and a strange hush hung in the air, as though it were waiting… waiting. Once, when he was a boy, he had seen the sea behaving like this, many years ago, just before an enormous tidal wave had hit this coast of Japan. He remembered that the sea had drawn back first, back until it couldn't be seen at all – and then suddenly it had stood up on end, an enormous wall of water that rushed towards the land, sweeping away villages and killing hundreds of people.

Their village was safe now, he knew that, built firmly on its cliff, but what about his friends on the beach? In the middle of all their fun they hadn't noticed what was happening to the sea – and even when they did they perhaps wouldn't realize what it meant. Any minute now the sea would turn, raise up and race towards the beach at tremendous speed, and they would all be drowned. He must warn them.

His legs were stiff now, after the exertions of the day, but he hobbled to the very edge of the cliff, cupped his hands round his mouth, and shouted. His voice carried out into the night but became lost when it reached the beach, smothered with the noise of music and dancing and singing. He shouted again, then realized that it was no good. They would never hear him. He looked beyond the dancers to where the sea was a single silver line on the horizon – there wasn't a moment to lose. It would take too long for his old legs to run down the cliff path and along the beach to the party. There must be a quicker way. Out of the corner of his eye he saw the torch still burning by his chair. He ran, faster than he thought possible, grabbed the torch and ran again. Past his house on the side of the village nearest to the cliff – to his barn, full of the dry golden grains that were to feed him through the winter.

Quickly he flung the torch through the door of the barn and then ran back as the flames leapt and spread, soon reaching high into the sky.

On the beach a young man saw the flames and shouted to his friends, pointing to the burning barn.

'Look, Yamacuchi's barn is on fire. Quickly, we must run and try to put it out.'

The dancing stopped, and the music, as everybody raced across the beach, anxious to help the old man. Then they were running, like ants, up the steep cliff path, the young ones leading the way, and the older ones coming as fast as they could. As the last one started the steep climb Yamacuchi glanced towards the horizon again. He saw a great gleaming wall of water, arched like some terrible monster ready to pounce – there was a second of silence, then a roar as it came racing towards the land.

Anxiously Yamacuchi looked to where the first of the villagers had gained the top of the cliff path. By now they too had seen the tidal wave and were helping the slower ones to safety over the edge.

There was a great leaping of foam and roaring of water as the wave hit the beach below, but by this time it was empty. Only the food and fires remained to be devoured by the waves.

The cliff seemed to shake with the fury of the sea, but the villagers were safe. They clustered round Yamacuchi, who had gone to sit in his chair, trembling with the fear that had just passed.

'You have given everything you have to save our lives. Now we will share what we have with you,' they told the old man. Yamacuchi nodded and smiled, content with what he had done.

7
Animal Fables

I just can't imagine a world without animals. So the animals
had to have a section of their own in this book.
There's an African story about the wise old spider Ananse.
Chicken Language comes from India. Long ago a man called
Aesop wrote a book of animal fables, and *The Mouse and
the Lion* is a modern retelling of one of those. There are
lots more too. And in all these stories the animals have
something to teach us humans.

Wisdom for Everyone

LAWRENCE DARMANI

Ananse the spider sat in the corner of his porch one sunny day. He was deep in thought because something was bothering him. He had been sitting there for over three hours, gazing at the blue sky and watching people pass by.

He was so deep in thought that he didn't see someone come out of the house and stand behind him.

'What am I going to do about this?' Ananse asked himself. Although he spoke aloud he didn't expect anyone to hear him. He was surprised, therefore, to hear someone ask him, 'Do about what?'

'Oh,' said Ananse, jumping from his seat and turning around quickly to see who it was. Ntikuma, his first son, stood by the door.

'You naughty fellow!' Ananse shouted. 'You almost scared me to death!'

Scared? Ntikuma was surprised to hear his father talk about being scared. He knew Ananse to be the bravest creature on earth. How could his father be scared? Was he not the only one in their village who could kill the python that destroyed their livestock?

Ntikuma asked his father, 'How can you be scared, Father? I thought you were the bravest one in our village.'

'I know,' Ananse replied.

'And you are the wisest creature on earth,' Ntikuma said.

'I know that, too,' Ananse replied. 'Now don't just stand there. See what your mother is doing and help her.'

When Ntikuma was out of sight, Ananse said to himself again, 'Yes, yes, I am the wisest one in the whole world. I know that!'

Ananse really believed that he was the wisest creature on earth. But instead of being happy, he was worried. He was worried because he didn't want anyone but himself to be wise. How could he protect all the wisdom on earth that belonged to him? That was the big question. Now what was the big answer? After Ntikuma left, Ananse sat for a long time in the corner of his porch that sunny day.

Suddenly he stood up and shouted, 'I've got it!' Now Ananse knew exactly what to do, but he didn't tell anyone. It was his secret.

One day Ananse told his wife and children that he was going to look for the tallest tree in the world.

'Why?' Ntikuma asked his father. But Ananse didn't tell anyone why. It was his secret.

Ananse searched through the forests, down the valleys, upon the mountains, and in the jungle. He searched for days and weeks and months and years. But he didn't find the tallest tree. Every time he found a very tall tree, he said to himself, 'No, this is not tall enough; people can climb this one easily and destroy my wisdom.'

Ananse had a secret plan. He wanted to remain the wisest creature on earth. He didn't want anyone else to share his wisdom. So he collected all the wisdom in the world and put it in a big brown gourd. He would hang the gourd full of wisdom on the tallest tree on earth. Then it would be safe.

One morning Ananse rose up just after the first cock had crowed. That was very early, but he didn't care about the cold. He took the gourd full of wisdom, hung it in front of him, and went out of the house. He didn't tell anybody where he was going. As he went, the gourd beat against his stomach.

Someone in the house saw Ananse go and followed him.

It was Ntikuma. He didn't want his father to know he was following him, so he followed quietly, at a distance. He followed him deep into the forest, wondering all the time what his father was up to.

At last, Ananse reached the middle of the jungle. There, standing straight into the sky, was the tallest tree on earth. It had taken Ananse many years to find it.

'Now,' said Ananse to himself, 'I'll hang this gourd of wisdom upon this tree, and no one shall see it or get to it.' He didn't know that his son Ntikuma, hiding behind a nearby tree, had heard him. Ananse hung the gourd in front of him and began to climb the tree.

But though he tried and tried, he could not climb the tree. Ntikuma watched from his hiding place, surprised that his father hung the gourd in front of him to climb the tree. All day, not stopping to eat or drink, Ananse struggled. But he could not climb the tree. The gourd pressed against his stomach and made climbing impossible.

'Father,' said Ntikuma calmly, 'I see you are trying to climb the tree. But don't you see that the gourd hanging in front of you is making it difficult for you to climb? Hang the gourd behind and you will surely be able to climb the tree.'

The wise father looked at his son. He was surprised to see him there.

'How on earth,' Ananse shouted, 'how on earth could you still have some of the wisdom that I've collected? And what are you doing here, you naughty boy?'

Fearing that his father would pounce on him, Ntikuma ran towards home.

Ananse the spider hated himself for showing how selfish he was. If he had succeeded in hiding all the wisdom, he would still be the wisest creature on earth. Everyone would go to him and he would do whatever he wanted with the people. But now he didn't know something as simple as hanging a gourd behind him to climb a tree. That meant he couldn't be the wisest creature on earth; he could not claim to be wiser than anyone.

Ananse was so angry that he smashed the gourd against the tree, breaking it into tiny pieces. A strong wind rose from among the trees and swept the tiny pieces away. That was how wisdom spread throughout the whole world.

The Fool and the Fox

From *The Discontented Dervishes – Persian Tales from Rumi*

ARTHUR SCHOLEY

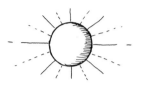

A holy man, who was journeying through a rocky desert on foot, came upon a sight that made him sad.

'Bless me,' he sighed, 'look at that poor fox lying there. It has no feet or legs. It must have been caught in a trap. Poor animal. Well, I hope the good God has pity on it, and ends its life soon. It certainly won't last long in that state.' And as there did not seem to be anything he could do for the fox, the holy man went on his way, shaking his head sadly.

A month later the holy man was returning the same way, and came to the spot where he had seen the fox.

'Goodness!' he cried. 'There is that fox – and it's still alive! Its fur looks healthy and how bright its eyes are. I can't believe it. How has it managed to survive?' But as there seemed to be no solution to the problem, he went on his way and soon arrived at the city where he lived. But the fox stayed in his mind, and that night he could not get to sleep for wondering about it.

'Perhaps I was deceived,' he thought. 'It must have been a mirage. On the other hand the fox looked real enough. Yet how could it live all this time? It is not able to hunt, and there is not a scrap of vegetation in that rocky place. It's a mystery! It may even be a miracle!'

Next day, when he should have been at his prayers or reading his holy book, he went on puzzling over the fox, until in the end he said, 'It's no good. I shall have to go and take another look.' So back he went into the desert and before long he was again gazing at the fox.

'It looks contented enough,' he said. 'I wonder if it will let me approach it?'

But just as he was about to make a move towards it, he jumped back in terror. He had seen a shadow among the rocks.

'God have mercy on me!' he gasped. 'It's a lion. It must have seen me. It will finish me off in no time.'

Quaking in fear, the holy man waited for the end. But after a few minutes passed and nothing happened, he peeped out from behind the rock. And now he saw what his terror had prevented him from seeing before: the lion had killed a jackal and had brought it to this spot to have its meal.

Soon the lion had finished. But there was still one chunk of meat left. The lion picked this up and dropped it in front of the fox.

'Well, now I know the answer,' said the holy man, 'but it seems more amazing than ever! If I hadn't seen it with my own eyes I wouldn't have believed it.' And his amazement was such that, next day, he could not resist coming out into the desert again. He hid behind the rock, and again the lion appeared with his kill, ate what it wanted, and left the rest for the fox to finish.

'It must be a sign from God himself!' cried the holy man. 'It's a message for me from the Almighty. From this time on I, too, will rely, like that fox, on the generosity of my creator. Yes, that is surely the lesson to be learned from this astonishing affair.'

He went home, gave away what few belongings he had, found himself a corner against a wall and settled down to wait.

'God will provide,' he said to himself. 'Like the poor fox, I will await the generosity of the lion.'

He sat there for several days and neither friend nor stranger came near. Several more days passed. Nothing happened.

'I'm getting weaker and weaker,' he gasped, 'and thinner and thinner. My bones are beginning to stick out. My skin is stretched so tight I'm in agony.' But still he sat. After a few more days of this he was too weak to move.

At last someone spoke to him. 'So this is where you are!' It was a friend, another holy man. 'Whatever is the matter with you? Are you ill? Why didn't you send a message?'

The holy man could only whisper: 'God sent me a sign, my friend. That is why I am here.' And slowly he managed to get out the story of the poor fox and the generous lion. 'Now tell me,' he ended, 'surely that was a sign from God himself?'

His friend burst out laughing. 'Of course it was a sign from God,' he roared. 'But how could you be such an idiot? Couldn't you see that you were supposed to imitate not the fox – but the lion?'

The Mouse and the Egg

WILLIAM MAYNE

Once a grandmother and a grandfather lived alone in a house high on a hill with a speckled hen who laid them eggs for tea, and a long-tailed mouse.

'I wish,' said Grandfather one day, 'I wish I did not always have a brown egg for tea. First there is the shell, and then there is the white, and in the middle is the yellow yolk, and that is all. I am tired of eggs. Can we have something better?'

The mouse heard and curled his long tail.

Grandmother heard. 'Oh,' she said, 'always be thankful. We have had the eggs boiled, we have had them fried, we have had them scrambled, and we have had them whisked in milk. What could be better?'

'I think,' said Grandfather, 'we could have a different sort of egg.'

The mouse heard that and straightened his tail.

Grandmother said, 'Go and ask the speckled hen.'

Grandfather went to ask the speckled hen in her house across the yard.

She said, 'I am sorry I do not please. You should have spoken sooner. Come back before tea and find whatever you find.'

The mouse heard and tied the first knot in his tail.

Grandmother heard. 'It had better be good,' she said. 'After all these years I can only cook eggs.'

Then Grandfather had a little sleep. The mouse watched him and tied the second knot. Grandmother set the table.

The speckled hen began to sing and call for Grandfather. She had laid an egg. He woke and crossed the yard to her and brought back what he had found.

It was a golden egg. The mouse saw and tied the third knot.

'My goodness, my gracious,' said Grandmother. 'A golden egg! What next?'

169

'What more could we want?' said Grandfather, and he put the egg on a cushion on a stool.

Grandmother said, 'I do not know; I declare I do not know, I cannot tell, how to cook a golden egg for tea: Should I roast or boil? Should I break the shell? Should I bake or coddle? Should I fry in oil? Or should I put it back again underneath the speckled hen to see how it will hatch?'

And the egg sat all alone and golden on the cushion on the stool. And the mouse undid a knot.

The wind blew and the door of the little house banged a little on its latch, and the golden egg began to crack.

The mouse undid the second knot, the fire spluttered in the grate, the smoke came in the room, and the golden egg began to break.

The mouse undid the third knot, because he knew, he knew. The soot came down the chimney and the wind banged in the sky, and the golden egg fell to dust.

'And that is what we get,' said Grandmother, 'after all your changes. That is the only egg we have, Grandfather. Are you hungry now?'

'I am,' said Grandfather. 'I could eat an egg.'

And the mouse curled his tail round and went to sleep, because he knew.

'I am sorry,' said Grandfather, 'sorry I spoke against my food. I shall not do it again.'

Outside, the speckled hen in her little house across the yard sang a song and called. Grandmother went out to her and found what she had to find, an egg, warm and brown and fresh.

'Thank you, speckled hen,' she said, and gave her corn and closed the door.

She went to her own house and closed the door.

Grandfather and Grandmother had an egg for tea.

'Thank you, Grandmother,' said Grandfather, 'for cooking my food.'

'Thank you, God,' said Grandmother, 'for giving it to us every day. Amen.'

'Amen,' said Grandfather, 'for the shell, for the white, and for the yellow yolk in the middle.'

'Amen,' said the mouse.

'Amen,' sang the speckled hen.

'Thanks Be to God'

FRED PRATT GREEN

For the fruits of his creation,
   thanks be to God;
for his gifts to every nation,
   thanks be to God;
for the ploughing, sowing, reaping,
silent growth while we are sleeping,
future needs in earth's safe keeping,
   thanks be to God...

For the wonders that astound us,
for the truths that still confound us,
most of all, that love has found us,
   thanks be to God.

The Troll and the Butterfly

From *The Troll and the Butterfly and Other Stories*

WILLIAM RAEPER

In a dark cave, in the jungle, in the heart of Africa, there lived a troll. He did not live in a friendly cave – the kind that keeps you cool in summer and warm in winter – the kind with dry stone walls and a sweet-smelling earthen floor – he lived in a dank, green, slimy cave that dripped water all the time down the back of his neck. It was always so cold inside the cave that the troll had to wear thick, woollen clothes.

Outside in the jungle the exotic flowers gasped for breath in the heat. Pink flamingos quivered on their matchstick legs as they looked for food in the lake. A hippopotamus yawned. A lion shook his tawny mane and roared. In this part of the jungle there were no men, only the troll.

But the troll was sad. 'I am fat, and ugly!' he cried. 'No one wants to be friends with me.'

Now the troll was a little fat as trolls go, but no one could say that he was huge. He had bright green eyes, bushy black hair, long teeth, and warts, but this is not unusual for a troll.

'I am fat and ugly!' he cried again. 'I'm horrible!'

He picked up his mirror and looked into it at his own reflection. 'Oh!' he shuddered, and put it down quickly again. He looked into the mirror so often that finally he could stand his reflection no longer. At last he smashed the mirror and wrapped the pieces in brown paper and buried them deep in the ground.

'Now I shall never have to look at myself again,' he said. But he felt worse than ever. The worse he felt, the more he ate and the more he ate, the worse he felt, because he got fatter and fatter.

Sometimes other trolls would come to visit him as they passed through the jungle on their way to the hidden mountains. But as all the troll in the cave ever talked about was himself and how terrible he felt, fewer and fewer stopped by, until at last they decided to leave

172

him alone. Some trolls, however, tried to offer him advice.

'Why don't you eat less?' they asked.

'I can't!' said the troll and shook his head. 'You don't understand!'

'Why don't you go out into the sunshine and sit by the lake?' they said.

'I can't!' said the troll. 'The world hates me!' and he shook his head. 'You don't understand!'

'You're not that horrible, you know,' some said.

'Oh, I am! I am!' said the troll. 'You don't know what it's like to be me. I'm going to be stuck this way for ever. Oh, you don't understand how bad that feels!' And the troll shook his head sadly from side to side.

'We can't help him,' said the other trolls. 'He must learn to help himself.'

So because the troll always talked about how fat and ugly he was, and how he would never change, and how terrible his life was, and because he would never let the other trolls speak at all, the other trolls left him alone. But that made him worse than ever.

'Nobody does like me!' howled the troll. And he howled so hard that the animals in the jungle thought a storm was coming and hid themselves under the trees.

After he was left on his own the troll left his cave as little as possible, but every day he had to go and find his dinner. He lived off juicy worms and grubs that he found under stones or on the undersides of leaves. That was proper troll food. This troll also ate leaves, twigs, rocks, earth and fungus – anything in fact that he could find when he was hungry.

When he went out to search for his grubs and worms, the troll took with him a big glass jar in which to put them. It was very old and precious and was his favourite possession.

The troll never went near the lake for fear that he would see his reflection in the water, but stayed in the thick of the jungle in the dark, green shadows of the trees.

One day he was just about to catch a big juicy grub, which he had just found under a stone, when a butterfly flitted through the trees and hovered in front of him.

'What do you want?' said the troll gruffly. 'Can't you see I'm busy?'

'I'm interested,' said the butterfly. 'What are you doing?'

'I'm catching my dinner,' said the troll, 'and if you're not careful I'll catch you!'

173

'Ha! Ha!' laughed the butterfly and sat down on a big, blue flower.

'Aren't you afraid of me?' asked the troll, astonished. 'Aren't I the ugliest thing you've ever seen?' And he gave a fierce roar that shook the jungle.

'Ha! Ha!' laughed the butterfly. 'I like you – you're funny!'

'You like me?' said the troll, even more astonished, for no one had ever said that to him before, not even his troll friends. 'You think I'm funny?'

The butterfly looked so free and happy that the troll became a little jealous. He thought of how miserable he was sitting in his damp cave all day with water dripping down the back of his neck, so that he grew sad to think that his new friend would fly away.

'You will come and live with me,' said the troll. And in a flash the butterfly was caught in the jar and the lid was shut tight.

'Help! Help!' cried the butterfly, but no one could hear him.

'Help! Help!' cried the butterfly again, but the troll only smiled a troll smile and said, 'We two can live together. I shall keep you dry and feed you and you can make me happy.'

Back in the cave the butterfly shivered inside the jar. He was the coldest he had ever been in the whole of his life. He heard the dripping water and saw the dank, green walls. 'How horrible!' he thought.

The troll clapped his hands. 'Make me happy!' he cried, but the butterfly only lay at the bottom of the jar and shivered.

'Maybe tomorrow then,' said the troll, a little disappointed, and he put a dark cover over the jar.

The following morning the troll woke up, yawned, stretched out his long arms and leapt out of bed excitedly. He pulled the cover off the jar and looked in at the butterfly. The butterfly was lying at the bottom of the jar; his wings were barely moving. It seemed that his colour had faded slightly.

'Make me happy,' said the troll.

'Just a little sunlight, just a little air and I will do what you want,' moaned the butterfly.

'But if I take you outside and open the lid of the jar, then you will fly away and I will never see you again,' said the troll.

'Oh, no! No!' said the butterfly. 'I won't do that!' But the troll did not believe him and put the cover back over the jar.

Even in the cave the butterfly heard the noises of the jungle through the cover and the jar. He heard the monkeys chattering in the trees and he heard the trumpeting of the elephants moving like slow, grey mountains along the jungle paths. He heard too, at night, the cry of the spotted leopard and the strange laughter of the hyena. Then he thought of how he used to be free and fly from flower to flower without a care in the world.

'My heart is sick,' thought the butterfly. 'I shall surely die.' And he felt so sick that he stopped moving altogether and his colour faded until he was quite white.

The troll continued to feed the butterfly and talk to him, for he was the only creature in the world whom the troll had to talk to. But gradually the troll began to feel guilty about what he had done to the butterfly and sorry that he had made him so unhappy – though the troll would still not let the butterfly go, because he was afraid of being on his own again.

One day the troll took the cover off the jar and saw that the butterfly was hardly breathing at all. The butterfly was white, like a corpse, and his eyes were half-closed.

'What is wrong?' asked the troll.

'My heart is sick,' answered the butterfly. 'I am going to die. When I am dead, please take my body to the lake and let it float away like a lily. That is my last wish.'

'Don't die!' pleaded the troll, and he began to cry big troll tears. 'If you die I shall be alone – and I have made you so unhappy!'

The troll peered into the jar and said softly, 'Is there any way left to save your life?'

'Just a little sunlight, just a little air and I may be well again.'

The troll thought long and hard. Finally he picked up the jar and walked out into the jungle. Through the trees he went, along the paths where the gazelles sprang and down to the lake where the animals went to drink. He put the jar down on a rock and tried to open it, but the lid was stuck.

'I cannot open the jar,' said the troll to the butterfly, but the butterfly was too ill to reply. The troll tried again. With all his strength he seized the jar and twisted the lid, but he could not open it. The lid had been on the jar for so long that it would no longer budge.

'I cannot open the jar,' said the troll again. 'What must I do?'

Now the jar was the most precious possession that the troll had, but he picked it up and broke it on the rock.

'Hold tight!' he said to the butterfly.

The jar smashed into many scattered pieces and the butterfly tumbled out. For a long time the butterfly lay on the ground and did not move. Then slowly the colour came back into his wings and they began to flutter. Suddenly he flew up and hovered in front of the troll.

'Thank you,' said the butterfly, and the troll laughed. 'Look!' said the butterfly and the troll saw for the first time in a long time his reflection in the water. He was laughing so much that he looked nicer than he had ever done before.

'You see,' said the butterfly, 'you're not very horrible. Thank you for thinking about me.'

The troll looked suddenly sad. His big green eyes filled with tears and he turned his head away.

'What's wrong?' asked the butterfly.

'Now you will go away and I will never see you again.'

'Nonsense,' said the butterfly. 'The jungle is my home and I will come to your cave every day and speak with you.'

Every day after that the troll and the butterfly had long walks together through the jungle. The troll spent more and more time out of his cave and eventually forgot how miserable he had been. He even made friends with some of the animals. He dried out his cave and put flowers in it and wrote to all his troll friends inviting them to stay. 'He has changed!' they said, and soon the troll had so many visitors and friends that he lived many long happy years in the jungle and never thought about himself again.

Chicken Language

A Story from India

E. SISLEY VINE

'He's out!'

Four young faces looked up with relief and joy as the little chick at last struggled free from his shell.

'Let's call him Struggle,' one said. So Struggle he became.

The chickens were the children's pets – so they almost all had names.

The previous day they had come from their school in the cool Nilgiri hills to spend the holidays at home on the hot South Indian plains. To their delight, they found that Henny had hatched yet another brood of chicks. Nine fluffy yellow heads peeped from under her black wings. From the tenth egg, yet to hatch, came a feeble cheeping.

Henny stayed on the nest with her chicks all that day, but when evening came she gave in to the clamour of the nine, and led them outside. The children pounced on the remaining egg, eager to help the imprisoned chick break free.

'No,' said Mother. 'He has to fight his own way out to grow strong. But we must keep the egg warm or he'll die.'

Carefully the children carried the egg indoors. They wrapped it in a woollen doll's blanket and set it on the dresser. The humid Indian nights were almost as hot as day. So even without its mother's warmth the little chick might live.

Sure enough, in the morning, the children were rewarded with a 'Cheep! Cheep! Cheep!' from the folds of the blanket, and they watched little Struggle break free.

'We'll have to give him back to Henny,' Mother said. 'She's the only one who knows how to look after him.'

Reluctantly the children agreed.

Henny accepted her chick without question. Under her wings

there was always room for one more.

'I have to go away for a few days,' their mother told the children. She had been learning a new language and was going to take an examination. 'Dad will look after you. And you must look after Henny and her chicks.'

'We will. We will. Don't worry,' they said as they waved her goodbye.

When she came home, a chorus of four excited voices greeted her.

'Henny has been teaching us chicken language!'

'Tell me about it.'

Four sharp shrill 'KWARKs' pierced her eardrums.

'That's the first word: "KWARK! KWARK!" '

'What does it mean?'

'It means "Come! Come at once!" She only says it once, and if the chickens don't come immediately it's too late.

'There were a whole lot of crows wheeling round in the sky, watching the little chicks. Henny cocked her head, keeping one eye on the crows and the other on the chicks. When she saw a crow swoop down she cried "KWARK!" We thought the little chicks would take fright and run away, but instead they all fluttered their little wings and ran to their mother as fast as they could.

'Henny stood with her wings spread ready to hide them. And as the crow swooped down she tucked her wings around them and they were safe. Just in time!

'Henny stretched her neck and pecked at the crow so that it flew away.'

'But Mummy,' said a tearful voice, 'Struggle's gone.'

'How did that happen?'

'The crows came back next day. We were indoors when we heard Henny's "KWARK!", and we ran out to look. Little Struggle had wandered further away from Henny than the others, and couldn't get back in time. A crow swooped down and carried him off.'

'Henny screeched at the crows and tried to beat them off with her beak. She nearly got her eyes pecked out! We thought she would be killed she tried so hard to save him.'

'Poor little Struggle.'

'Yes. We cried. If only Struggle had come at once.'

That mother hen knew more than her chicks, the children's mother thought to herself. She saw the danger – they didn't. If only her chick had obeyed at once...

But the children had more to tell her about the new chicken language they had been learning.

'Then there's "PLOK! PLOK! PLOK! PLOK!" You must say it quickly, and puff out your lips.'

' "PLOK! PLOK!" What does *that* mean?'

'It means "Come and eat – your dinner's ready!" '

'The little chicks were running about, pecking at this and that. But they couldn't find much to eat. Then Henny saw a great big fat cockroach running across the yard, and she ran after it. She caught it and broke it into little pieces with her beak. Then she called "PLOK! PLOK! PLOK!" and they all came running and pecked up the bits.'

'All the time they were busy pecking at the ground Henny stood with her wings spread out to give them shade from the sun and hide them from the crows. Her wings make a shadow.

'The chicks run around all day, and every time Henny finds something for them to eat she calls "PLOK! PLOK! PLOK!" and they come running. They love red ants. They're always hungry!'

'But look how they're growing,' Mother said.

'At midday, when it's hottest, Henny says, "OOM! OOM! OOM!". That means "Follow me", and she leads them to the shade of the banyan tree. She sits, and they all hide under her wings and have a rest.

'But Henny doesn't sleep. She's watching out for them all the time. Sometimes she talks to them.'

'What does she say?'

' "WAUK! WAUK! WAUK!" '

' "WAUK! WAUK!" Is that right?'

'No, not like that. You must say it slowly, and as you say it you rub your chin on your neck and pretend the chicks are under your wings.'

'What does it mean?'

'It means "I love you." '

'Where is Henny now?'

'Oh, she takes her chicks to bed at sunset. Come and see!'

The older hens went to roost every night in an outhouse. The door was locked against four-footed jackals, two-footed thieves, and slithery slidey snakes. But Henny had her own apartment – a large packing-case put up on blocks. A sloping piece of timber served as a ladder. Up this ramp Henny led her brood every evening, single file. They came at once in answer to her 'OOM! OOM! OOM!' If they followed her, they were safe.

The children and their mother made their way to the packing-case. The hatch was still open, so they could see the chicks jostling one another to see who could get closest, under Henny's wings.

'Listen!'

They heard Henny's gentle 'WAUK! WAUK! WAUK!' and the cheerful 'Cheep! Cheep! Cheep!' of the chicks.

'What are they saying?' Mother asked.

'They're singing for joy, and thanking Henny for looking after them!'

That night there was no need for a bedtime story.

'WAUK! WAUK! WAUK!' Mother said softly, as she turned down the light in the kerosene lamp.

'WAUK! WAUK! WAUK!' came the sleepy reply. 'We love you too.'

The Mouse and the Lion

From *Aesop's Fables*

RETOLD BY BOB HARTMAN

The mouse skittered left.

The mouse skittered right.

The mouse skittered round the rock and under a leaf and past the dark wide mouth of a cave.

And then the little mouse stopped. Something had grabbed his tail. The mouse wrinkled his nose and twitched his whiskers and turned around. The something was a lion!

'You're not even a snack,' the lion yawned as he picked up the mouse and dangled him over his mouth. 'But you'll be tasty, nonetheless.'

'I'm much more than a snack!' the little mouse squeaked. 'I'm brave and I'm clever and I'm stronger than you think. And I'm sure that if you let me go I will be useful to you, one day. Much more useful than a bit of old bone and fur that you will gobble up and forget.'

The lion roared with laughter, and the little mouse was blown about by his hot breath.

'Useful? To me?' the lion chuckled. 'I doubt it. But you are brave – I'll give you that. And cheeky, to boot. So I'll let you go. But watch your tail. I may not be so generous again.'

The mouse skittered left.

The mouse skittered right.

The mouse skittered away as quickly as he could, and disappeared into the woods. Hardly a week had passed when the lion wandered out of his cave in search of food.

The lion looked left.

The lion looked right.

But when the lion leaped forward, he fell into a hunter's snare! The ropes wrapped themselves around him. He was trapped.

Just then the little mouse came by. 'I told you I could be useful,' the little mouse squeaked. 'Now I shall prove it to you.'

The lion was in no mood for jokes. He could hear the hunter's footsteps. 'How?' he whispered. 'How can you help me, now?'

'Be still,' said the mouse. 'And let me do my work.'

The mouse began to gnaw. And to nibble. And to chew. And soon the ropes were weak enough for the lion to snap them with a shrug of his powerful shoulders.

So, just as the hunter appeared in the clearing, the lion leaped away into the forest, with his new friend clinging to his curly mane.

They returned to the cave as the sun fell behind the hills. 'Thank you, my friend,' said the lion to the mouse. 'You are indeed clever and brave, and you have been more useful than I could ever have imagined. From now on, you have nothing to fear from me.'

The mouse smiled.

Then he skittered left.

And he skittered right.

And he skittered off into the night.

The Story of Charlotte the Caterpillar

From *Mrs Gatty's Parables of Nature*

RETOLD BY PAT WYNNEJONES

One lovely summer day a fat, green caterpillar was quietly lumbering along a cabbage leaf. Her name was Charlotte.

She had not gone far when she came across a white butterfly fluttering feebly beside a little pile of eggs.

'Oh dear, kind caterpillar, do please help me,' gasped the butterfly. 'I feel so ill. I think I shall die. Then what will become of my baby butterflies? Won't you please take care of them for me?'

Before Charlotte had time to think of an answer she went on. 'You must be very careful what you feed them on when they hatch out. None of your coarse cabbage leaf. Oh, dear! I can't think why I laid them in such a horrid place! No, you must give them early dew and honey from the flowers. And don't let them fly far before their wings are really strong… be kind to them…'

Then the butterfly died, leaving Charlotte standing beside the eggs feeling very worried indeed.

'Fancy asking me to look after baby butterflies!' Charlotte said to herself. 'They'll fly away as soon as they hatch out. They won't bother with me!'

For she had no idea that the eggs would not hatch into butterflies, but into caterpillars like herself. Poor Charlotte! She did not know that a caterpillar must turn into a chrysalis and then into a butterfly. She did not know the wonderful order of things. She only knew what it was to be a caterpillar, crawling along. But she had a kind heart and made up her mind to do her best.

That night she had no sleep, she was so anxious. She made her back ache, walking round the eggs to see they came to no harm.

In the morning she had an idea. 'I must find someone to help and advise me,' she decided. 'Two heads are better than one.'

But whom should she ask? There was a dog in the garden, but he was so playful and rough. He would probably sweep the eggs away when he wagged his tail. The cat liked to bask in the sunshine under the apple tree and sleep. She was much too selfish to bother about them.

'I'll ask the lark,' she decided. 'He goes up so high, and no one knows where he goes. He must be very clever indeed.'

Charlotte could only crawl. She could never go up high – so that was her idea of perfect glory.

The lark lived in a cornfield nearby. Charlotte sent him a message asking him to come and talk to her. When he came she told him her problem and asked him how to feed the little creatures she thought would be so different from herself.

'Perhaps you can ask about it next time you go up high,' she suggested timidly.

The lark only said he might. Charlotte watched anxiously as he went flying up into the bright blue sky, singing as he went. Higher and higher he flew, until she could hardly hear a sound. She could not see him, for it was difficult for her to look upwards. She could only rear herself up, very carefully. But she soon dropped down again, to walk round and round the eggs, nibbling a bit of cabbage leaf now and then as she went.

'What a time he has been!' she said to herself. 'I wonder where he is just now! I would give all my legs to know!'

Charlotte took another turn round the eggs. 'He must have gone up higher than ever this time. I wish I knew where he goes and what he hears in that strange blue sky! He always sings as he goes up and as he comes down, but he never gives any secrets away.'

At last the lark's cheerful voice was heard again. Charlotte almost jumped for joy as she saw her friend descend with hushed note to the cabbage bed.

'News, news, glorious news, my friend,' sang the lark. 'But the worst of it is, you will never believe me!'

'I believe everything I am told,' said Charlotte hastily.

'Well, then, first of all I will tell you what these little creatures are to eat,' – and he nodded his beak towards the eggs. 'What do you think it is to be? Guess!'

'Dew and the honey out of flowers, I'm afraid,' sighed Charlotte.

'No such thing, old lady! Something simpler than that – something you can get at quite easily.'

'I can't get at anything but cabbage leaves,' she replied sadly.

'Well done! You have found it out,' cried the lark joyfully. 'You are to feed them on cabbage leaves.'

'Never!' said Charlotte indignantly. 'It was their mother's last request that I should do no such thing!'

'Their mother knew nothing about it,' persisted the lark. 'But why ask me, and then not believe what I say? You have no faith or trust.'

'I believe everything I'm told,' replied Charlotte.

'No, you don't,' answered the lark. 'You won't even believe me about the food, and that's only the beginning of what I have to tell you. Why, what do you think those little eggs will turn out to be?'

'Butterflies, of course,' said Charlotte.

'No! Caterpillars!' sang the lark, 'and you'll find it out in time.' And off he flew, for he didn't want to stay and argue with his friend.

'I thought the lark was kind and wise,' Charlotte mused as she wandered round the eggs again, 'but he's silly. Maybe he went up too far this time. But I'd still like to know where he goes and what he does,' she added aloud.

The lark heard her as he came down again. 'I'd tell you if you'd believe me,' he sang.

'I believe everything I'm told,' the caterpillar repeated, as solemnly as if it were true.

'Then I'll tell you something else,' sang the lark, 'the best news of all! You will one day be a butterfly yourself!'

'Nonsense!' exclaimed the caterpillar. 'Don't tease me! Go away! I won't ask your advice again!'

'I told you you wouldn't believe me,' said the lark sadly.

'I believe everything I'm told,' Charlotte began again, 'at least...' she hesitated, 'everything sensible. But to tell me that butterflies' eggs are caterpillars, and then become butterflies! You are too wise to believe such nonsense, lark! You know it's impossible.'

'I know no such thing,' retorted the lark. 'When I hover over the cornfields or soar up into the heavens I see so many wonderful things that I see no reason why there should not be more. Oh, Charlotte, it is because you crawl, because you never get beyond your cabbage leaf that you call anything impossible!'

'Rubbish!' shouted Charlotte. 'I know what's possible or impossible, as well as you. Look at my long green body and those endless legs – and then talk to me about having wings and being a butterfly! It's ridiculous!'

'You're ridiculous,' the lark retorted, 'trying to reason about things you don't understand. Don't you hear how my song swells with joy when I soar up to that mysterious wonderworld above? Can't you take what I hear, as I do, on trust?'

'That is what you call…'

'Faith!' interrupted the lark.

'How can I learn faith?' asked poor Charlotte.

At that moment she felt something at her side. She looked round – eight or ten little green caterpillars were moving about and had already made quite a hole in the cabbage leaf! They had broken from the butterfly's eggs!

Charlotte was filled with astonishment – and then with joy. For since one wonder was true, perhaps the others were too.

'Teach me your lesson, lark!' Charlotte would say when the lark came down to the garden. And the lark would sing about the wonders of the earth below and of the heaven above.

The caterpillar talked for the rest of her life to her friends about the time when she would be a butterfly. But none of them believed her.

Charlotte had learnt the lark's lesson of faith, and when she was going into her chrysalis grave, she said, 'I shall be a butterfly some day.'

Her friends laughed at her, but she didn't care.

And when she was a butterfly and was going to die again, she said, 'I have known many wonders. I have faith – I can trust even now for what shall come next!'

P.S.
One Day...

I began my story collection right at the beginning, when the
world was newly-made. That's a very long time ago, and the
world is getting old now. So will it wear out? Will the spoiling
destroy it? Will it go on for ever, or will it come to an end
some time? That's quite a scary thought. But it needn't be.
For the Bible says that one, wonderful day everything in our
tired old world will be made new again. That's what
these last few pages are about.

The Lion and the Lamb

RETOLD BY PAT ALEXANDER

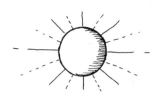

*This story comes from the Bible, the book of Isaiah,
chapters 9, 11 and 65.*

Long ago, in the land of Israel, there was a prophet called Isaiah.
His special job was to be God's messenger. That's what a prophet is.
And Isaiah loved God enough to do as God said, even when no one
wanted to listen.

Those were terrible times, with a lot of wars and fighting. God's
people felt he couldn't be looking after them any more if he let those
awful things happen. It seemed as if their troubles would never end.

But this is the message Isaiah brought from God to cheer them up:

> *'When everything seems dark*
> *you will see a shining light*
> *A child will be born*
> *– a new king for my people.*
> *"Wise Counsellor" he will be called,*
> *and "Prince of Peace".*
> *He will be just and fair.*
> *There will be peace in his kingdom for ever.*
>
> *'One day, all the hurting will stop.*
> *You will all know me*
> *and I will never leave you.*
> *The wolf will not hurt the lamb,*
> *and the lion will eat straw like the ox.*
> *The calf and the baby bear*
> *will go to sleep together*
> *– and little children will take care of them.*
> *One day, I will make the whole world new.'*

No More Tears!

RETOLD BY PAT ALEXANDER

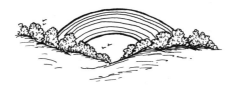

This story comes from the very last book of the Bible, Revelation,
chapters 21 and 22. Many centuries have passed since the prophet
Isaiah spoke of God's new world. Jesus has come into our world
and lived and taught and died. Now his followers are telling
everyone he's alive again, come back from the dead; that he's God's
own Son who died for us; that he is the 'new king', the 'Prince of
Peace' Isaiah said would come, whose kingdom goes on for ever.

John looked across the sea to the mainland. He could see it clearly.
If only he were free. If only he wasn't a prisoner on this island, he'd
be over there telling everyone about Jesus, just as he'd been doing
ever since Jesus left them. John was an old man now. And it was
telling people about Jesus that had got him into trouble. Some had
welcomed John's good news, but others had objected. There was
trouble. And the soldiers came and marched John away.

On his island, lost in thought, John jumped at the sound of a
voice behind him. He turned – and what he saw then was like a
dream, a whole series of dreams, one after the other, scene after
breathless scene. There was God on a great throne, with his angels
round him. Then John saw a lamb (he knew it was Jesus) and all
God's people. He saw what would happen at the end of the world,
just as if it was going on then and there, right before his eyes. It was
wonderful, amazing, terrible; with trumpets and horsemen and
battles, and evil defeated for ever. Then it was over, and all the people
who ever lived were standing before God to account for what they
had done. Now at last the world was made new, with nothing left to
spoil it.

John saw a golden city, bright and shining. Its great jewelled gates
stood always open for people of every nation to come and go. There
was no sun or moon, yet it was brighter than the brightest day, with

a light that shone out from God himself. Down the middle of the great central street ran a river, crystal clear, with a tree of life on either side. Those trees bore fruit every month of the year, and their leaves were for healing.

And John heard these words:

> *'Now all the people will be God's people*
> *and he will live with them.*
> *He will wipe every tear from their eyes.*
> *There will be no more dying or crying or hurting.*
> *Those things are all past.*
> *This is God's new world.'*

'Garland for Tomorrow'

ANNE BELL

Leave behind dark wreaths of sorrow
and twine the earth and all its streams
with birdsong and a twist of leaves,
tie them together with a knot of dreams –
and hold fast.

Acknowledgments

Thanks go to all those who have given permission to include material in this book, as indicated in the list below. Every effort has been made to trace and contact copyright owners. We apologize for any inadvertent omissions or errors.

'The Making', 'The Spoiling' and 'The Flood – and a Rainbow' from *My Own Book of Bible Stories*, copyright © 1983 and 1993 Pat Alexander, published by Lion Publishing. 'The Little Things' and 'Garland for Tomorrow', copyright © Anne Bell. 'High Tide' by Margaret Bell, 'The Oak' by Stuart Little, 'Sonnet' by Catherine Richards, 'A Shetland Prayer' by Janine Riley, 'The Toad' by Helen Southwood and 'Thoughts of a Seed' by Ben Thackeray, Andrew Pimblott, Paul Armstrong, Lauren Eves, Roger Twiss, David Cross and Richard Jones, copyright © Turning Heads Theatre Company. 'The Eyrie' from *Eagle Boy*, copyright © 1986 Rodney Bennett. 'Switch on the Night' by Ray Bradbury, reprinted by permission of Don Congdon Associates, Inc. copyright © 1955, renewed 1983 by Ray Bradbury. 'The Black Fox' from *The Midnight Fox*, copyright © 1968 Betsy Byars, published by Faber and Faber Ltd. 'Debbie, Sandy and Pepe' by Merrill Corney from *The Best Present and Other Stories*, copyright © 1990 Albatross Books Pty Ltd. 'Wisdom for Everyone', copyright © Lawrence Darmani. 'The Little Black Rabbit' from *Shadrach*, copyright © 1953 Meindert DeJong, published by The Lutterworth Press. *The Very Worried Sparrow*, copyright © 1978 Meryl Doney, published by Lion Publishing. 'The Lost Princess' from *The Snow Goose*, copyright © 1941 Paul Gallico. Reproduced by permission of Aitken & Stone Ltd. 'I Hole Up in a Snowstorm', from *My Side of the Mountain* by Jean Craighead George. Copyright © 1959 by Jean Craighead George, renewed 1987 by Jean Craighead George. Used by permission of Dutton Children's Books, a division of Penguin Books USA Inc. 'The River' from *The Wind in the Willows* by Kenneth Grahame, copyright © The University Chest, Oxford, reproduced by permission of Curtis Brown, London. 'Thanks be to God' by Fred Pratt Green, copyright © 1970 Stainer and Bell Ltd, Victoria House, 23 Gruneisen Rd, London, N3 1DZ. 'The Mouse and the Lion', copyright © 1998 Bob Hartman, from *The Lion Storyteller Bedtime Book*, published by Lion Publishing. 'Yamacuchi's Harvest', copyright © Peggy Hewitt. 'Angel Train', copyright © Nan Hunt. 'The Founding of Narnia' and 'Digory, the Witch and the Apple' from *The Magician's Nephew* by C.S. Lewis, repro-duced by permission of HarperCollins Publishers Ltd. *Big Tree, Little Tree* by Sylvia Mandeville, copyright © 1979 Lion Publishing. *The Mouse and the Egg* by William Mayne, copyright © 1980 William Mayne, published by Lion Publishing. Reproduced by permission of David Higham Associates. *Kippy Koala and the Bushfire*, copyright © 1985 Win Morgan, published by Lion Publishing. Copyright permission granted by the author. 'Haffertee and the Picture Pattern' from *Haffertee Hamster Diamond*, copyright © 1977 Janet and John Perkins, published by Lion Publishing. 'The Troll and the Butterfly' from *The Troll and the Butterfly and Other Stories* by William Raeper, copyright © the estate of William Raeper. 'The Rain', copyright © Jenny Robertson. 'The Lion's Tale' from *Tales from the Ark*, copyright © 1993 Avril Rowlands, and 'Noah's Tale' from *More Tales from the Ark*, copyright © 1995 Avril Rowlands, published by Lion Publishing. 'A Drop of Water', copyright © 1987 Fay Sampson. First published in the *R.E. Today Assembly File*. 'The Cat, the Monk and the Prince' from *Pangur Bán, the White Cat*, copyright © 1983 Fay Sampson, published by Lion Publishing. *Zilya's Secret Plan*, copyright © 1978 Ulrich Schaffer, published by Lion Publishing. 'The Fool and the Fox' from *The Discontented Dervishes – Persian Tales from Rumi*, copyright © 1977 Arthur Scholey, published by André Deutsch. 'The Pigeon' by Jean Selby from *Goodnight Stories* compiled by Meryl Doney. First published 1982 by Pan Books Ltd. 'Sam and the Hacker' from *Here I Am!*, copyright © 1992 Russell Stannard, published by Faber & Faber Ltd. 'What in the World is the Wide, Wide World?' by Norman Stone, copyright © 1979 Lion Publishing. 'My Dad', 'Who Made a Mess?', 'The Naming of the Animals' and 'I Like the World' from *The Day I Fell Down the Toilet and Other Poems*, copyright © 1996 Steve Turner, published by Lion Publishing. 'Chicken Language', copyright © Elizabeth Sisley Vine. 'The Old Man and His Children', 'The Old Woman and the Bear' and 'The Reluctant Raindrop', copyright © Jean Watson. *The Story of Charlotte the Caterpillar*, copyright © 1984 Pat Wynnejones.

MIR OBS